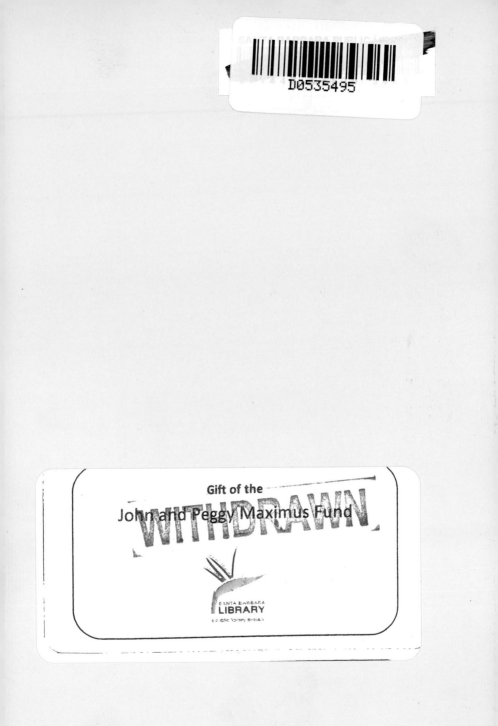

My Life in Smiley:
SAVE ME!
(or don't . . .)

Acknowledgments

Many thanks to Clémentine Sanchez for her invaluable help, Alexandra Bentz for her trust, Samantha Thiery for her support and management, as well as the entire Smiley team.

 For Elisa and Hortense.

For Lola, who always had a smile on her face.

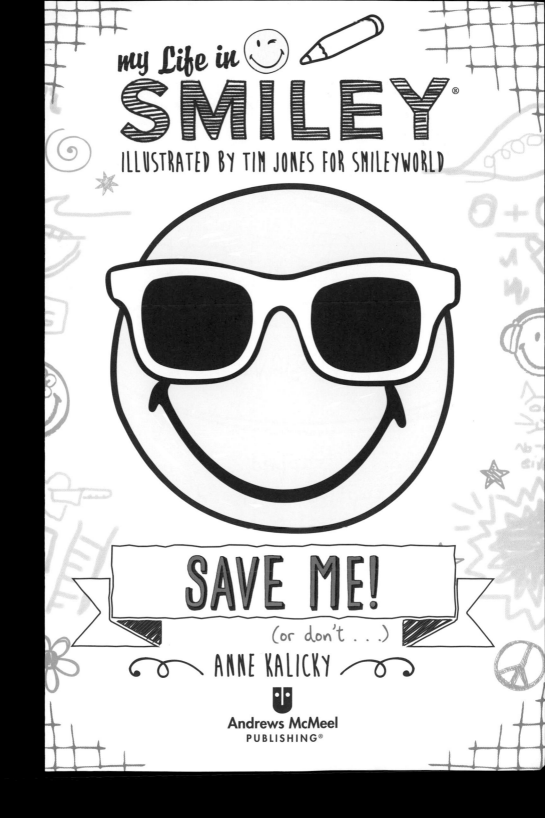

my Life in

SMILEY®

ILLUSTRATED BY TIM JONES FOR SMILEYWORLD

SAVE ME!

(or don't . . .)

ANNE KALICKY

Andrews McMeel
PUBLISHING®

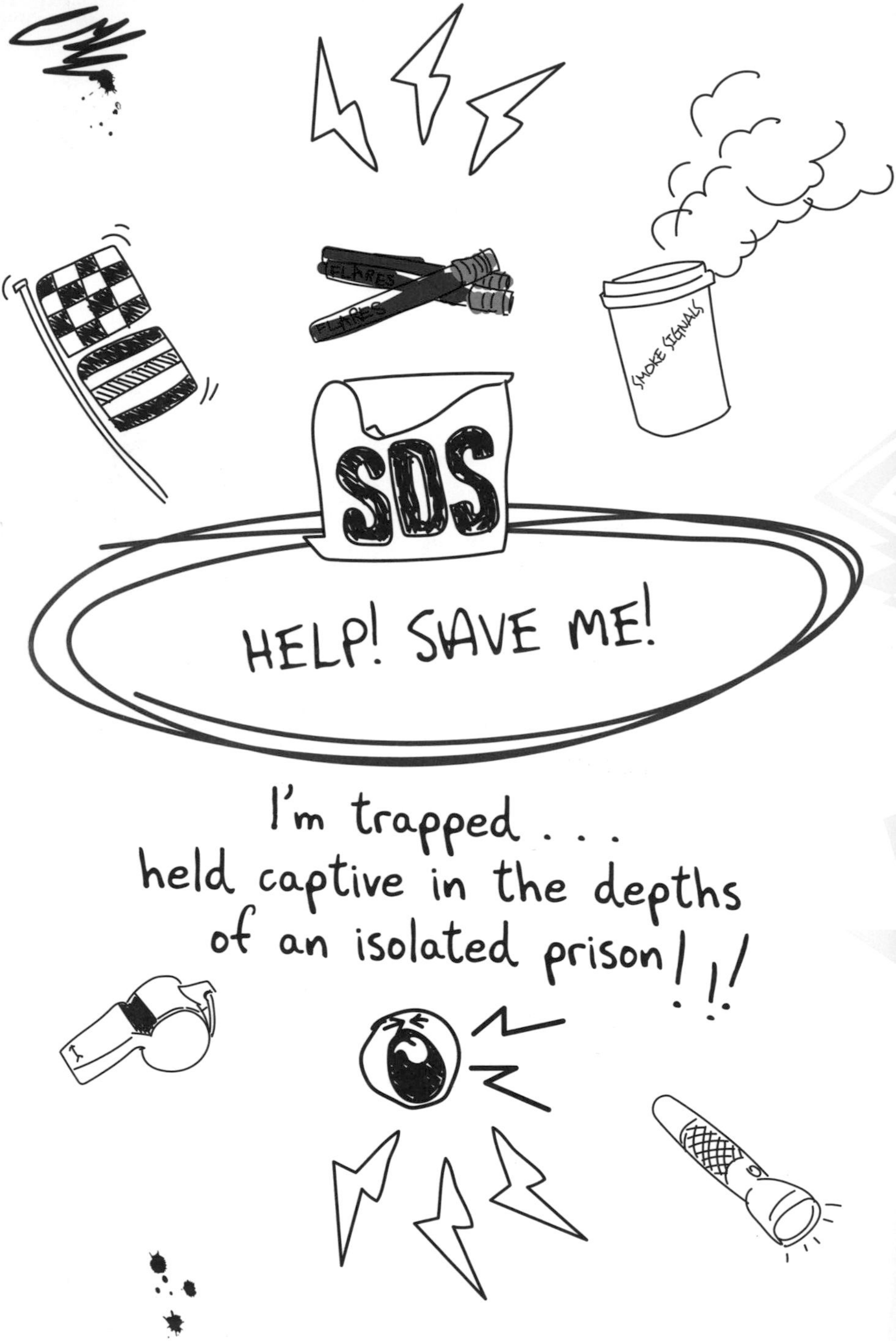
FLARES
FLARES
SMOKE SIGNALS
SOS
HELP! SAVE ME!
I'm trapped . . .
held captive in the depths
of an isolated prison!!!

The heat here is unbearable. My pen is trembling. I'm writing in the dark, with only the faint glow of a flashlight to guide me. All I've got in my backpack are a crushed chocolate bar, salt and vinegar chip crumbs, and two pieces of Atomic candy for my ENTIRE "sentence." I'm not alone, but—at the time I'm sending out this distress call—I don't even know if my fellow prisoners are still human. At night, they seem to transform into strange creatures, because I hear horrible snoring and growling all around me. But I can hardly bring myself to describe the worst thing of all. . . . It . . . smells like moldy socks! I can barely breathe—I'm suffocating! To whoever is now reading these desperately scrawled lines: come rescue me! Don't let me rot here. If I get out of this nightmare alive, I promise to be your eternal servant. Whatever you do, do it fast. I don't know how long I can hang on!

5

DAY 1
Saturday Night

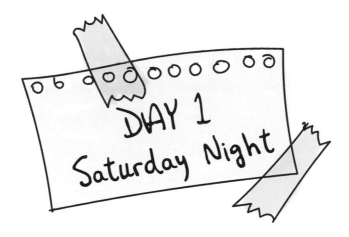

Dear future  human,

Believe it or not, I'm stuck here . . .

at SUMMER CAMP for TWO LOOOONG WEEKS! You heard me! I swear it's not a joke! I'm sure you're already wondering how such a thing could happen to me, Maxime Cropin the Great! Well honestly, I'm asking myself the same thing. . . . I guess I'd have to go back to the end of the school year, which was probably the best year of my entire life. Everything was going perfectly, thanks to my innate genius (obviously)—but also thanks to my best friends Tom and Nico, the success of our fundraiser for Welcoming Wheelchairs, and my kiss with Naïs, who's the prettiest girl in our grade and ended up being CRAZY ABOUT ME. Remember all that from my diary last year?

Yeah, it's hardly been more than a week . . . but I have the feeling my best days are already behind me. I was planning to stay on cloud nine for the rest of my life, but things went right down the tubes when my parents decided, on a whim, to send me to . . .

CAMP!

I almost gagged when I heard the news. Me? At camp? Honestly, do I look like I'm cut out for summer camp?

Life just isn't fair, especially after all the work I put into seventh grade  (like the Reading Passion club, remember?). I was expecting to just "chillax" with Tom and Nico all July, before joining Naïs in Brittany . . . at Grandpa Joff and Grandma Ragny's house. This is the biggest disappointment in my nearly thirteen years of existence!

Ever since, it's like my life's been in black and white.

I should have suspected something fishy was going on. Now I remember hearing my parents whisper, when I was too busy with the It's All Good stuff, about supposedly giving me more "autonomy," "responsibility," "sociability," "y," . . . "y," . . . more "y," . . . and who knows what other fantasy my parents came up with.

I think I'm developing a phobia for words that end in "y," because they NEVER mean anything good. My mom told me again and again that it was an "incredible" 🙂 opportunity, and you know why? It was all because the Champ Camp brochure said it was a

FIVE—SUN HAT
RESORT !

I should explain that, for years and years, I've listened to my dad's stories about being in the military. And believe me, all of his anecdotes about impeccably made beds, waking up at five in the morning, peeling potatoes, scrubbing toilets, shaving heads—you know, stuff meant to "toughen you up"—didn't do a thing to make me want to go to camp. Adults should think more carefully before they speak. Anyway, I tried absolutely everything to talk them out of it.

But there was no way out of this mess, and before I knew it, it was time for me to leave.

I don't know if I'm going to survive. I'll need to summon  SUPERHUMAN courage and patience OF STEEL.

So that's how I found myself on a bus this morning, nose pressed up against the window, watching my parents smile 😊 and wave at me as they shrunk—a spot, a black smudge, a single point, then nothing. It was clear that I was, beyond any doubt, in deep trouble.

Then the horrible feeling of being an astronaut floating in empty space came back, ☹ times three thousand. Future human, I bet that light years from here, in the distant future, you guys don't have summer camps anymore. Teenagers are taken care of by super babysitter robots, 🤖 or better, they have little spacecraft to carry them from one planet to the next whenever they get bored. Boredom probably doesn't even EXIST in your time. But you can see that during mine, things are far from being that simple.

I had a lump in my throat, and it took all I had to hold back my tears  and keep from looking like a sissy.

So here I am completely and utterly stuck. BUT I've made up my mind to do NOTHING whatsoever to mingle with this group of caged hamsters or to participate in camp "activities." Maybe you think I'm being tough? Cruel, even? Well I'm only exaggerating my misery a tiny bit!

By the way, once I finally got on the bus, I went into stealth mode. In other words, I used the hoodie tactic. Heard of it?

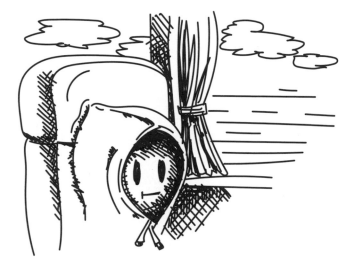

You pull the hood of your sweatshirt or jacket down over your nose, pretend to sleep, and avoid talking to anyone.

Even better: put your headphones on (even if you're not listening to anything). And the most drastic method: let your hair grow long enough to cover your eyes. Your pick!

My tactic proved effective for the first three minutes . . . until the seat next to me lurched as if a mammoth had just sat down in it. Then I heard a voice with a strange accent say: "Hey-a! My-a name ees Aldo, but my-a friends call me the prankmaster!"

From the very first second, I didn't like this "Aldo" kid one bit. He seemed just as dumb as Raoul Kador, if you know what I mean.

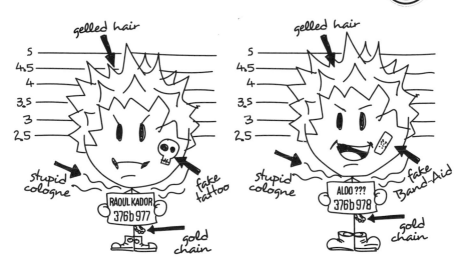

gelled hair

5
4.5
4
3.5
3
2.5

stupid cologne

RAOUL KADOR
376b 977

fake tattoo

gold chain

gelled hair

5
4.5
4
3.5
3
2.5

stupid cologne

ALDO ???
376b 978

fake Band-Aid

gold chain

For the first part of the trip, he claimed to be the only person IN THE WORLD to have "glow-in-the-dark boogers." 😮 Then he started sticking them all over the seat in front of him. 🤢

But at one point, we went through a really dark tunnel and I saw that his boogers weren't glowing at all. 😐 So when the bus made a pit stop, I changed places and sat down next to Valentin, a really skinny pale dude. During the ride, the counselors introduced themselves: their names are

Caroline and Anthony.

That's how I learned there were twenty-five of us "kiddos" in this same predicament, heading toward Montlardons. Mom must've already told me a dozen times, but I was so shocked by the "leaving immediately" part that I guess I didn't pay attention. At first glance, there seemed to be more boys than girls on the bus—which made me even <u>LESS</u> excited.

Gerald, the camp director, was also on board. To be honest, he didn't exactly seem easy-going. After counting and recounting us about twenty times, he reminded us that we weren't allowed to have <u>phones</u>, <u>video games</u>, or anything else that resembled twenty-first century <u>technology</u>.

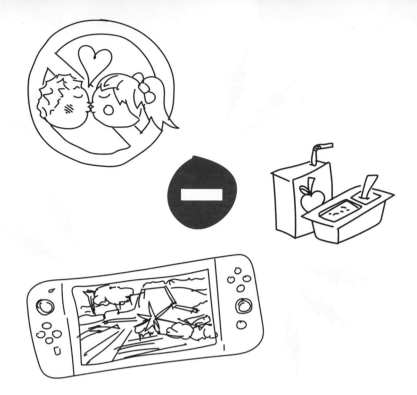

And he said if he caught anyone with them, there would be "serious consequences." TWO WEEKS without screens to look at or buttons to click. . . . This is going to be terrrrrible!

But you know what? The one bit of good news is that the packing list for camp said we were allowed to bring an "observation notebook."

That's absolutely perfect, because I know a thing or two about notebooks! But I know what you're thinking: what if someone stumbles upon the masterpiece that you alone, dear future human, hold in your hands???

That's why, before leaving, I dipped into my savings and spent some of the money Grandma had given me for Christmas to buy a . . . secret pillow! I bet you're wondering what that is. It's a pillow—but not really a pillow. It actually has a hidden zipper that you can open to stash things inside. You remember Lisa, my little sister? She's the one who gave me the idea. She's had one for a year: a Smiley face pillow, her favorite! By the way, it looks a little like the fluffy heart pillow that I gave Naïs at her party last year. . . .

Anyway, mine is even cooler. I hid my journal inside, locked it, and poof—out of sight, out of mind.

The bus ride felt endless, and we arrived just before dinner. Before we could even catch our breath, Gerald called everyone into the activity room to remind us AGAIN about inside rules . . . and even outside rules.

Then he made
an announcement
that totally
freaked me out. →

First of all, you'll
all be receiving "the
mark of the camp."

There's no way
they're going to brand
me like a cow or give me
some Champ Camp tattoo
for the rest of my life!

Actually I think
I panicked a little
too soon, because
they just passed
out camp "swag."

Then he gave us our bunk assignments and showed us around the property. He asked us to unpack our stuff and then regroup in the "mess hall." We had exactly twelve minutes to put away our "gear," as my dad would say.

All aboard to Champ Camp!

PACKING LIST

14 pairs of underwear

14 pairs of socks

2 pairs of pants

5 pairs of shorts

1 sweatshirt

6 T-shirts

1 jacket

2 sets of pajamas

1 hat

1 pair of tennis shoes

1 formal outfit

1 pair of sunglasses

1 bag of toiletries

1 observation notebook

We went to our cabins, and as soon as we took off our socks, the room instantly smelled like moldy cheese!

But THE WORST thing was that when I opened my bag, I realized all my clothes were covered in <u>GLITTER</u>. My mom had come up with the brilliant idea to wash Lisa's princess costume with MY camp stuff, and all of the glitter had stuck to my clothes!

Just one more thing that's going to keep me from being incognito here . . .

I guess the camp swag came along at just the right time.

Then we heard a jarring whistle blow, practically loud enough to burst your eardrums. It was Anthony, the group leader for the boys, calling us to dinner.

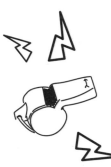

The smell in the dining hall wasn't much better than the cabin. I still can't decide whether it was spoiled fish or more of a fermented kidney. And for that matter, do I really have to describe the thing that ended up on my plate? Actually, I can't do it. Thankfully, I remembered I had a couple of chocolate bars in my backpack . . . at least, that's what I thought until I checked.

I ended up at a table with Dylan, a super strong and athletic guy who seemed happy to be there. There was a kid named Samuel too. He's the oldest—seventeen—and you're not going to believe it. . . . He's been coming here for ten years! A serious feat, if you ask me.

Medal of honor →

All of the girls had gathered together except one, Salomé, who joined our table. I was terrified Aldo was going to sit down next to us, but luckily he took a spot somewhere else. Later, I saw him empty his plate into his table's water pitcher. So that meant no one sitting with him could drink a single drop. As for me, I didn't open my mouth during the entire meal.

Afterward it was time for "newbie night," something else I frankly could've done without. ☹ They packed all of us strangers into a small room like sardines. We made a circle, and Caroline and Anthony sat down in the middle. Anthony was holding some kind of stick. At first I was scared to death—I thought we'd done something wrong and were about to get punished.

For a second, I was wondering if my parents might've made some mistake and signed me up for a boot camp for juvenile delinquents. ☠ But I calmed down a bit when he explained it was the "talking stick." The idea was to simply introduce yourself and then pass the stick to your neighbor.

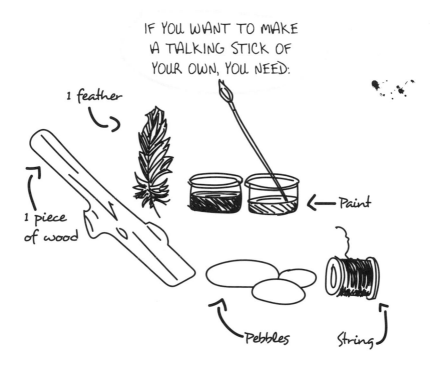

IF YOU WANT TO MAKE A TALKING STICK OF YOUR OWN, YOU NEED:

1 feather

1 piece of wood

Paint

Pebbles

String

There you have it, something that could prove pretty useful at home when Marion hogs all of the attention at dinner. She's so annoyyyying! I can't believe neither of my sisters had to go to camp!

And to think people are always going on and on about gender equality! That's nothing but mumbo jumbo.

LIFE ISN'T FAIR!

Anyway, Anthony spun the talking stick around on the floor, and it stopped on me! I was forced to introduce myself, breaking my promise not to participate in any camp activities. I should also say that my mouth was totally sore from gritting my teeth for so long. 😬 But apparently everyone here is deaf . . . or else I wasn't trying very hard to be heard.

Next it was everyone else's turn. Jules, the cranky kid, wouldn't stop scratching his shoulder blade. Coline, the chatty girl, took at least ten minutes more than everyone else. Valentin explained that he's afraid of spiders. Romain, the foodie, was nibbling on a piece of bread as he spoke, so we didn't understand a thing. I noticed that Clara was looking at me. Clara, she's pretty—but not as pretty as Naïs.

Finally, Aldo introduced himself: he's a fifteen-year-old Italian kid. 🙂 He couldn't stop himself from adding that he was born with a distinctive characteristic: "an-a eextra bicep," the "aldocep," and that's why he was stronger than everyone else. Show-off! 😎

At 9:30 it was time for curfew. Phew! I was happy to go back to my cabin and have some breathing room, well . . . so to speak. All I can do now is count the days.

DAY 1 SATURDAY	DAY 2 SUNDAY	DAY 3 MONDAY	DAY 4 TUESDAY	DAY 5 WEDNESDAY	DAY 6 THURSDAY	DAY 7 FRIDAY
DAY 8 SATURDAY	DAY 9 SUNDAY	DAY 10 MONDAY	DAY 11 TUESDAY	DAY 12 WEDNESDAY	DAY 13 THURSDAY	DAY 14 FRIDAY
DAY 15 SATURDAY						

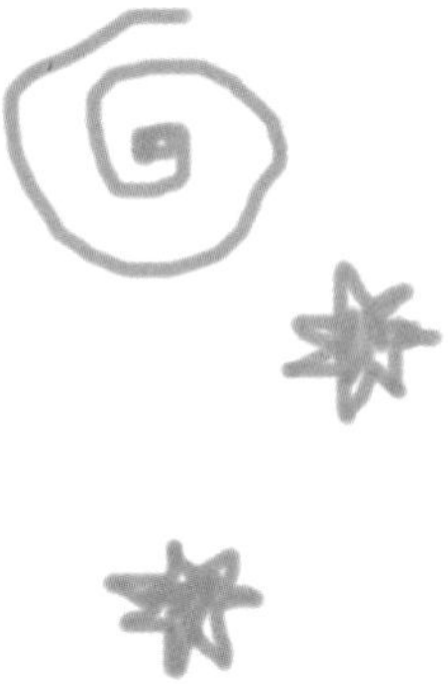

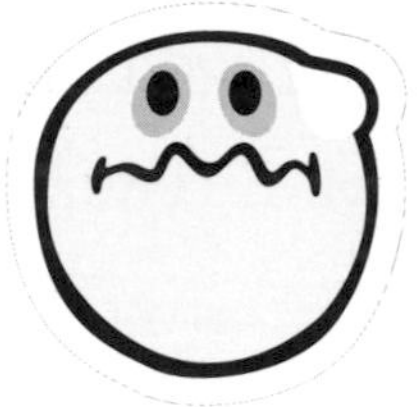

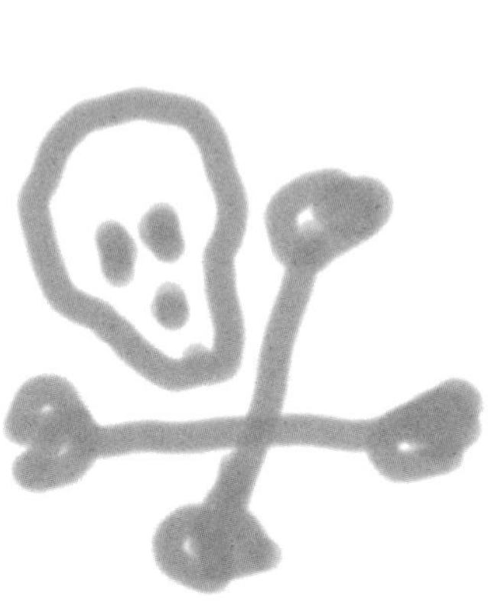

DAY 2
Sunday

Last night was horrible: I couldn't get a wink of sleep! 😦 When I'm not at MY HOUSE in MY BED, I have a hard time adapting. You know what I mean, dear future human? And ever since I found that furry blanket in the basement last Christmas, it's even worse. I've become totally addicted to that thing. WITHOUT IT? I can't sleep anymore. 😦

It's also partly because of Yanis. He's in the bunk above me, and the whole night he kept tossing and turning every which way, mumbling in his sleep. The metal bedframe was so squeaky!!

Ah! I forgot to tell you about my roommates. So there's Mehdi, Maxence, and Yanis. We haven't had the chance to talk much yet.

There are four of us in a five-person room. In other words, we're enjoying a little luxury: an extra empty bed. 😊

First, I was thinking it's pretty chill to just have four people.

Second, Aldo is in the cabin's OTHER room, and I'm not going to complain!

On the other hand, I just learned something that didn't exactly cheer me up: more hamsters like us are thrown into this cage <u>every week</u>! Some go, others come. I realized that in a week, I'll have to "make friends" with twice as many kids. And that doesn't sound like good news to me. Anyway, I'm trying not to think too much about it for the moment. 😖

Thankfully, Anthony explained that there's not a set time for everyone to wake up, since Champ Camp lets everyone "sleep at their own pace." 😴

Result: I woke up at ten o'clock, and when I got to the dining hall everything was already cleared away! 😞 Since lunch yesterday, my stomach's been PRACTICALLY EMPTY except for a few pieces of chocolate and some salt and vinegar chip crumbs at the bottom of my backpack.

I was
WEAK,

SO WEAK!

The kitchen was empty. I had absolutely NO idea where the leaders and the other campers were. Yes, counselors are sometimes called "leaders," in case you were wondering, future cyber-noob.

That floating astronaut fear almost came back, but in the end I just went back to my cabin for a little nap. Before hitting the hay, I took advantage of being alone to shake out my glitter-covered clothes over the empty bed. Then as I was falling asleep, after about five minutes, I heard a weird noise in the hallway. So I went out to take a look, but there was nothing. I thought I'd had an auditory hallucination like at Conrad's house, when his sister was talking on her cell phone. I went back to my room, and the sound started again! So I went back out and heard it coming from the bathroom. You wouldn't believe it, but just as I got closer to the door, I noticed the handle moving all on its own! I knocked on the door and asked if anyone was inside. A quiet voice answered.

Uhhh... I'm stuck inside. Can you call for help?

It was Valentin, the guy I sat next to on the bus. I had to go around to all of the buildings to find Gerald's office. I explained the situation to him. He didn't look too surprised—he just walked right out with his toolbox. It must not have been the first time something like this had happened, which I think is totally 😠 outrageous. In any case, we went to go rescue Valentin.

It turns out he was trapped in the bathroom for over an hour, and since he was embarrassed, he didn't want to call for help. Everyone else had gone to archery, so he'd decided to take care of things himself by trying to break the lock with the toilet brush. . . . 😬

Epic fail! Long story short: ever since this little episode, Valentin thinks I'm his savior and won't let me out of his sight. 

Later that morning, a new guy arrived. And I thought everyone was already here! Guess what—he missed the bus yesterday, so his parents had to drive him all the way here. . . . Mom and Dad? PARENTS??? PARENTS!!! To tell you the truth, we were all super jealous 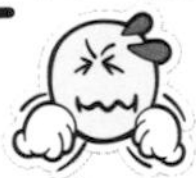 that this kid got to have another twelve hours with his family (which means twelve fewer hours in this rat hole). It made the whole camp depressed when we saw his parents leave. I think it's going to be especially hard for Valentin to get over it.

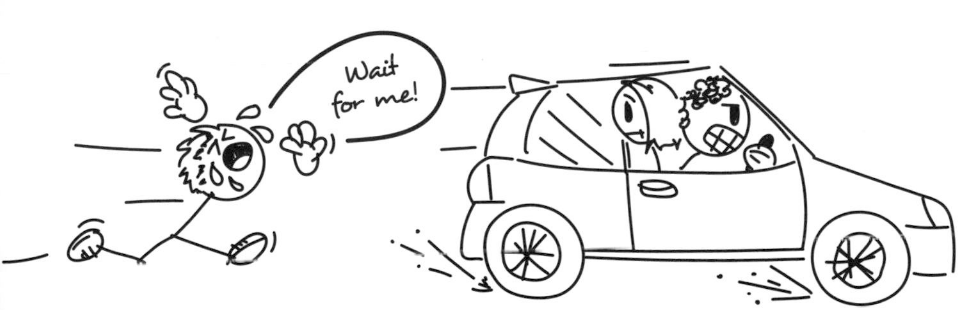
Wait for me!

In less than a minute, there was <u>practically</u> a riot, and Anthony, our counselor, was totally overwhelmed by the situation. . . . It was at that moment I realized I had absolutely no idea how many miles away from home I was.

When school starts again,

I've really got to step up my game in geography class.

Anyway, things calmed down once we heard the lunch bell.

Let's just say the new guy isn't going to win any popularity contests anytime soon. While waiting for their food, everyone started chanting for the talking stick so he could introduce himself. His name is Killian, he's thirteen and seems like he's permanently asleep. Aldo was yelling at him: "Coo coo? Signore Killian! Anyone home?" He didn't get any dessert.

That meant an extra bowl of ice cream for us!

And believe it or not, but the empty bed in MY room is now occupied by Killian. Figures! I should have known. So long comfort, luxury, and privacy. Then I remembered that I'd shaken out my glitter-covered clothes over his bed, which I wasn't too proud of now.

Since participating in anything at this camp was still

OUT OF THE QUESTION,

I snuck away to my cabin after lunch. But after fifteen minutes, Mehdi, one of my roommates, came to tell me that the leaders were looking for me everywhere. . . . It was time for board games. I told him I didn't feel like it and wanted to be left alone.

I guess I came off a little strong, but this guy seemed pretty nice and funny after all. Then Anthony himself came to find out what was wrong. He'd noticed since this morning that I'd been VOLUNTARILY keeping to myself.

I was toast, megatoast.

He gave this long speech about the joys of community, sharing, friendship, team spirit, and the wonderful memories that I would have from my time here —even if it was tough to fit in at the beginning.

"All this is normal," and blah blah and blah blah blah. I say it's baloney! I wondered for a second if he might've written that little book my mom has, *Children Soft as Pandas*, because his tone and style were the exact same. He reminded me that I have FIFTEEN DAYS and that I won't be able to stay cooped up the whole time. I already knew all that. Why hit me right where it hurts, huh? To make him go away, I told him I needed "some time to think about it." It worked, because he ended up leaving. But he added one final guilt trip: "As you wish."

After a while, the silence and solitude started getting to me,  and all of a sudden I felt a huge void. Nothingness, black holes, eternity, infinity . . . it was the astronaut fear! I felt a tear run down my cheek. I was breaking down inside. Then I thought about things for a while and took a nap. When I woke up, I had a brilliant idea:

PRETEND!

That was the solution!!! Pretend to participate, pretend to eat, pretend to talk—maybe even pretend to have fun.

We'll see. May as well take advantage of these two weeks to develop my skills as an actor. So I (pretended) to join everyone in the dining hall for dinner. Aldo opened his mouth to make one of his lousy jokes, but Samuel flicked him on the nose. I (pretended) to sit down at the table with my roomies, and I swallowed an enormous piece of chocolate cake . . . uhh, that part wasn't pretending.

DAY 1 SATURDAY	DAY 2 SUNDAY	DAY 3 MONDAY	DAY 4 TUESDAY	DAY 5 WEDNESDAY	DAY 6 THURSDAY	DAY 7 FRIDAY
DAY 8 SATURDAY	DAY 9 SUNDAY	DAY 10 MONDAY	DAY 11 TUESDAY	DAY 12 WEDNESDAY	DAY 13 THURSDAY	DAY 14 FRIDAY
DAY 15 SATURDAY						

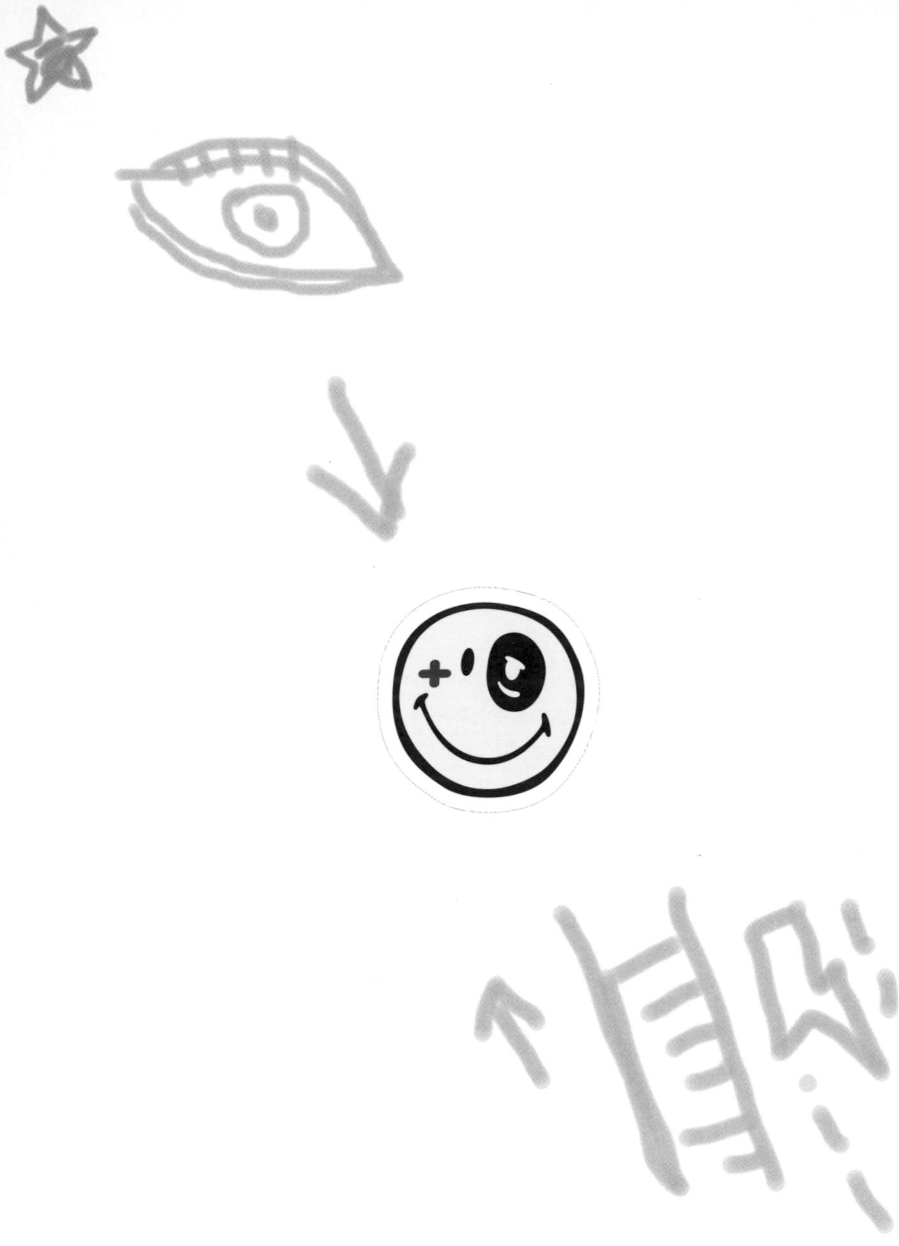

DAY 3
Monday

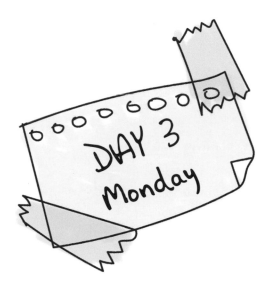

Today it rained cats and dogs. That makes
TWO DAYS we've been cooped up inside. 😫
I'm wondering if my parents might be better
off just picking me up and getting their money
back. I figured we'd at least have free time
or something, and I'd be able to get some rest.
After:

- overcoming my hunger,

- saving someone trapped in
  the bathroom,

- barely avoiding a riot,

- and playing the part of "happy camper,"

I could at least allow myself the luxury of
another nap—but ABSOLUTELY NOT. As
it happens, Anthony and Caroline organized
some matches of Werewolf. Everyone had
to participate, and I wound up on a team
AGAINST MY WILL, once again!

The game went like this: each player got the role of either a <u>villager</u> or a <u>werewolf.</u> The goal was for the villagers to find and kill all of the werewolves, and the monsters had to eliminate all of the villagers. When the leaders explained the rules, deep down I was actually kind of excited. It sounded totally scary, and you know how I love spooky stuff! But you can bet I didn't show one bit of enthusiasm. I just . . . pretended!

The counselors dimmed the lights, and we started the round. I got the role of the witch: she had control over the life and death of the other players, which suited me just fine.

The game was really cool, but I saw Aldo cheat by opening his eyes to see who was a werewolf and who was a villager, even though that's AGAINST THE RULES.

Afterward, we played a round of Champ Camp bowling. It's just like regular bowling—except the only equipment is people. And guess what, I was immediately chosen as a "pin" along with Nathan, Jules, Mehdi, and Lola. Aldo was thrown at us, and we all ended up on the ground . . . strike. After ten minutes, the game of Champ Camp bowling turned into heavy-metal mosh pit. Gerald had to step in before half of the campers ended up with missing teeth or broken limbs.

After dinner, we regrouped in the activity room for the camp song. Oh yeah! I forgot to mention that Anthony and Caroline taught us the camp's tune last night—which is way less rock 'n' roll than a chaotic game of Champ Camp bowling, if you ask me. I get the feeling we'll be singing it every night, and I'm not exactly excited about that. I plugged my ears, pretended to sing, but there was no hope. . . . The tune was still stuck in my head!

Summer's finally here, now it's time to cheer.
We're here at Champ Camp, so let's stomp and stamp.
We have so much fun, in a blink it's done,
When it's time to go, we'll say "Awww, no!"

I still think they're trying to make us
believe camp is great, but I'm not convinced yet.

Later on in our room, I have to admit I had a lot of fun with Mehdi, Maxence, Yanis, and Killian. Mehdi started a burping contest to "lighten the mood." Believe it or not, but he burped the ENTIRE alphabet! We were laughing so hard my sides hurt!  Then we just chatted for a while. Right off the bat, we talked about middle school, teachers, friends, girls . . . and we all agreed that camp is totally dumb!

DAY 4
Tuesday

I had trouble sleeping again because of Yanis: he flips around like a pancake EVERY night, 😔 and it sounds like he's chanting some kind of spell for rain and bad weather.

Want to know why? Because the leaders want to take us HIKING! I think Yanis is like me: he was hoping for a much cushier summer. His trick seemed to be working though, because since we arrived the weather has been lousy. . . . I'm secretly thanking him for it, by the way. 😊

But this morning our luck ran out:
a blindingly bright sun shone through the
window! Luckily for me, Tom and I had become
interested in environmental protection, survival
skills, and all that stuff several years ago. It's
all because of the TV show *The Lone Survivor*.
We learned how to cook grasshoppers and boil
water in a tree stump with hot stones. We
even started a club called Extreme Explorers.
At the time, we made our classmates who

JÉRÉMY TROUILLON

wanted to join pass "initiation"
trials. But besides a few
sunburns and stiches, the results
weren't very conclusive.

NOLAN LATOUCHE

MATTEO CULOCHE

In fact, except for Tom and me, no one ever succeeded in getting into our club. Back then my dad also loaned me his book, *The Resourceful Ranger's Handbook*. And believe me, ever since then I've known a thing or two about how to survive all alone in "a hostile environment." All that's to say that I tried to reassure Yanis about the hike, but he wasn't the least bit thrilled by the thought of having to trudge through the woods. 😊

Then we went to get breakfast. That's when I discovered with HORROR that the waffles we'd been gulping down since Sunday were made from a plastic container full of a suspicious yellowish liquid. 😖 Dear future human 🔲, I should tell you that I CAN'T HANDLE plastic containers ever since the day we visited Aunty Pom-Pom on vacation.

As a snack, she offered me some cookies that she'd been keeping in a big beige/ murky yellow plastic box . . . the kind of containers she bought in sets of twenty from infomercials. But after eating a few, I watched her offer the exact same box to Sassy, her dog—who shoved her slobbery snout inside. And so I never knew if Sassy had eaten the same cookies as me . . . or if I'd eaten her dog treats!

Long story short, we got ready and left for Montlardons BY FOOT! What they didn't tell us was that we had to travel almost ten miles there and back. It was a good thing we didn't know that ahead of time, because otherwise I think there might have been a spontaneous outbreak of bubonic plague in the camp to avoid going.

After about fifteen minutes, Valentin
started complaining that his feet
hurt, and then it was Lola's
turn. Then again, she'd worn
pink glittery tennis shoes
that were apparently
two sizes too
small for her.
Thankfully, the
counselors had made sure to
bring the first-aid kit.

At one point, we wound up on top of a huge hill. That's when Aldo suggested we do a "shoe race." This is originally an English game. 🖤 Conrad evidently forgot to mention this tradition, but the idea is to roll a large wheel of cheese down a hill and sprint down to catch it. Since Aldo didn't have any cheese on hand, he used his shoes instead. Before the leaders could say anything, he threw them. The whole group shouted and hurled themselves down the slope. . . .

I admit that in the midst of all the excitement, I didn't have much of a choice. I closed my eyes 😣 and took off too. And believe me—this time it was impossible to pretend. But what no one had really anticipated was that, since it had rained a ton yesterday, the ground was like an ice rink. We all slid and rolled all the way down.

I had no clue what was happening since I kept my eyes shut the whole time. I swear! I totally ate it! I really regretted acting before thinking it through, because once I rolled to a stop, I was covered in grass and mud! But all of a sudden, I saw Clara heading straight for me. Instinctively—and because I'm so classy  —I caught her in my arms, and her face stopped about two inches from mine . . . maybe even less.

Aldo was worse off: he managed to lose his shorts as he was hurtling down the hill! Mehdi put them on top of his head and imitated Aldo: "Hey-a! Look at my-a crown! I'm-a the Prankmaster!"

I couldn't stop myself from laughing with everyone else  . . . unlike the counselors. When they caught up to us, they REALLY scolded us. They said what we had done was incredibly dangerous and we were lucky no one got hurt. Then we spent a good fifteen minutes looking for Aldo's shoes before we got on our way again—in total silence.

Around noon, we reached a river where we stopped for a picnic. That's when Anthony and Caroline split us up into "patrols."

CHOW PATROL:
- Max
- Aldo
- Maxence
- Clara
- Lou

TABLE AND CAMP PATROL:
- Sarah
- Gabriel
- Quentin
- Jessica
- Mehdi

SUPERVISION PATROL:
- Dylan
- Nathan
- Romain
- Hugo
- Mélissa

WASHING PATROL:
- Coline
- Lola
- Fanny
- Killian
- Yanis

KINDLING PATROL:
- Samuel
- Valentin
- Jules
- Maeva
- Salomé

I thought I'd be able to catch my breath a bit, but I was wrong again. I wound up preparing wood-fired pizzas for TWENTY-SEVEN PEOPLE! 😮 Other patrols were responsible for starting the fire, setting the table, cleaning our dishes, and "supervising" us. Valentin seemed completely relieved to not be in Aldo's patrol, but he came back from the woods with splinters all over his hands. 🙁

Dear future human, I'll confess to you that the pizzas, even though a little burned, were seriously delicious. We even made chocolate dessert pizzas. A delicacy! 😋 I'd never eaten anything like that before. It really cheered me up!

After the meal, the leaders suggested some "discussion time" all about our "dreams." We were asked to imagine what we'd be like in twenty years.

Salomé wants to become a pilot. Fanny's gonna be a billionaire. Samuel is going to become a professional kite surfer. Hugo said he'll have at least three Niphon 92s, and he'll be a professional video game player. 😊 Nathan wants to win the Nobel Prize, but he doesn't know what for yet. Lola is going to be Miss Universe and a camp director—at the same time! And Aldo predicted, in all "modeesty," that he'll be "president-ay!"

I thought about everything I could tell them. I'd live on Eratosthenes, a new planet, because we will all have had to evacuate an uninhabitable Earth by then. I'd live in a 3D-printed house with ultra-high speed internet and a whole pile of remotes. I'd work from my bed, thanks to the holograms and robots that would do everything for me. I'd have tons of salt and vinegar chips delivered to me by drones.

I'd be super healthy because of antimicrobial cells placed all over me. I'd fly my own spaceship, and—above all—I'd be famous thanks to my notebook.

But instead I just told them I actually don't daydream that much. I just live life as it comes. Obviously that didn't really sweep them off their feet! Well I won't score any points with that response, especially with the girls. 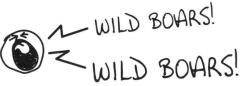 It was at that exact moment that we heard strange noises, like snorts. . . . Aldo jumped to his feet in a single leap and yelled:

— WILD BOARS!

— WILD BOARS!

In the chaos that followed, Valentin put a pan over his head to protect himself, and everyone jumped into the river. A bath was kind of overdue, in my opinion, because we were still totally dirty from the shoe race earlier. 😱 Even Anthony and Caroline jumped in. But once in the water, we scanned between the trees and didn't see a single boar charging at us. It turns out Samuel had pranked us! Believe me, he really got us with that one!

So then I had an idea that I whispered to Mehdi, Maxence, Killian, and Yanis—my bunkmates. We dove under the water and acted like crocodiles. We tickled Samuel's legs, and he totally freaked out! He jumped around in all directions and everyone burst out laughing, most of all the girls.

By the way, I noticed Clara looking at me again. I get the feeling she likes me, but I may just be imagining things. And besides, Naïs is waiting for me back in Brittany. . . . In short, we had a GREAT TIME! We splashed around for at least two hours, until Aldo started shouting that the current was taking him away. He had started to drift a bit, but he wasn't actually in trouble since he could still touch the bottom! Once he realized this, he turned bright red.

The counselors whistled for us all to come back. We gathered up our stuff and headed back to Champ Camp. The hike back didn't feel as long to me. Once we got back, we quickly showered, got ready for bed, and then went down to the dining hall to gulp down something that reminded me of my dad's "mixed salads"—but in a soup version.

I'm journaling early tonight, because there's no evening activity. It goes without saying that we're too tired. . . .

Pffffff . . .

Whatever . . .

Zzzzzz . . .

~~DAY 1~~ ~~SATURDAY~~	~~DAY 2~~ ~~SUNDAY~~	~~DAY 3~~ ~~MONDAY~~	DAY 4 TUESDAY	DAY 5 WEDNESDAY	DAY 6 THURSDAY	DAY 7 FRIDAY
DAY 8 SATURDAY	DAY 9 SUNDAY	DAY 10 MONDAY	DAY 11 TUESDAY	DAY 12 WEDNESDAY	DAY 13 THURSDAY	DAY 14 FRIDAY
DAY 15 SATURDAY						

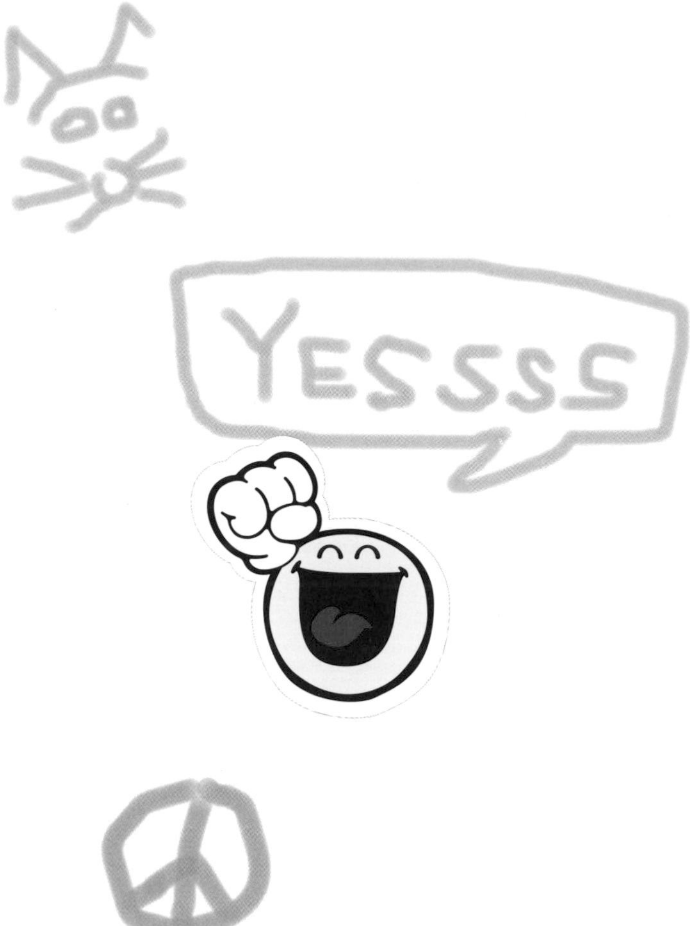
YESSSS

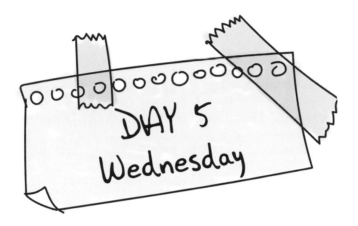

DAY 5
Wednesday

Dear future human,

I have absolutely no idea how I fell asleep last night. The last thing I remember was hearing Mehdi imitating a boar . . . or maybe he was already snoring. After that I had a crazy dream. I was on board a spaceship. My copilots were Tom and Nico, but they had antennae on their heads. We were going through multiple dimensions to escape the camp. . . . It was one creepy dream!

But this morning I almost had a panic attack, because guess what: I couldn't find the key to my secret pillow! It bothered me all breakfast long. Afterward, I said I needed to go to the bathroom, so I'd have an excuse to run back to my cabin while everyone met for activities.

I slipped away and took advantage of the opportunity to search everywhere. I found things under the beds that must've been forgotten from years past.

Then I noticed something shiny way in the back, near the wall. Since my arms weren't long enough to reach it, I went to look for a broom. I pulled the thingamajig out with the handle. You aren't going to believe me: it wasn't my key, but an ANONYMOUS notebook with a silver padlock!

I tried to open it, and the lock jumped ... as if by magic. But the only thing inside was disappointment! The pages were absolutely blank! ☹

All of a sudden I heard footsteps in the hallway, and I stashed the journal under my pillow. It was just Anthony coming to look for me, and I had to follow him. What was I going to do with this diary? I needed some time to think it over. 💡

Today Caroline and Anthony organized a scavenger hunt. I didn't like the sound of it, because I remembered one time, when I was younger, my mom had organized an Easter egg hunt with the parent-teacher organization. At the time, she'd taken a break from work to focus on raising us and helping out with school events.

About fifty people were supposed to participate, but my mom ended up overdoing it on the whole door-to-door promotion thing. <u>Result:</u> way more people showed up than expected. And they all showed up at eight in the morning, when the hunt was supposed to begin at two. The crowd started losing their patience, and after a while people totally flipped out and knocked over the fences. It turned into a mad rush to collect as many eggs as possible.

And on that very same day, my mom decided to go back to work.

Anyway, we had to organize into five teams, but Valentin ended up all alone. So ~~I kindly offered~~ I (pretended) to tell him to join our team.

Caroline and Anthony passed out the list of things to look for all around Montlardons. Finally some good news! We could expand our boundaries! Freedom!

I was starting to feel pretty cooped up in this camp.

THINGS TO FIND FOR THE SCAVENGER HUNT

☐ One of Aldo's shoelaces

☐ The population of Montlardons

☐ An earthworm

☐ The name of the butcher's dog

☐ The distance between city hall and the church

☐ A used ticket from the train station

☐ The geographic coordinates of the Baltic Bistro

☐ The exact definition of "deoxyribonucleic acid"

☐ The answer to this riddle: how many drops of water can you put into an empty glass?

☐ A paperclip necklace

We figured out the riddle right away—did you? The answer is only one drop, because after that the glass isn't empty! But the rest of the game took all day, because Aldo's team was the first to find the paperclip necklace. It was on the fridge in the dining hall, and this moron wore it around his neck for the entire scavenger hunt!

Since we spent practically the whole day looking for the necklace, we at least had a chance to find out more about Montlardons and the butcher's dog (his name is Roast).

Then we bumped into the mayor, who gave us some free candy. What a guy! Clara, Valentin, Mehdi, a few others, and I took our bag of treats to the local park. Believe me—after these last few days of hardship, I would have gladly eaten even moldy candy! But I'd never tasted anything so sweet in my entire life. Life was worth living again!

At first we just sat around and grumbled about Aldo. He may have had an "eextra aldocep," but he was clearly missing a few brain cells, or at least it seemed that way. 😵 I decided to take this opportunity to explain IAG and the Welcoming Wheelchairs fundraiser I'd done with Nico and Tom. They seemed really impressed . . . especially Clara. It's crazy how much girls like good deeds! 😉

But talking about Nico and Tom again suddenly ruined my mood. Mehdi must've noticed something was off, because he whispered a joke in my ear.

Why did the lemon fail its driving test? Because it kept peeling out!

😄 I chuckled, and as everyone else continued talking, I whispered to him that I'd found an empty notebook this morning in our room. But I'd barely finished my sentence when we saw Anthony running toward us. He looked super worried. Apparently everyone had been looking for us for half an hour. Gerald was about two seconds away from calling the police. We must have hung out in the park for a little too long. . . . We went back to camp pronto and took our showers.

After dinner, it was "challenge night." We'd known that was the evening activity since it was posted on the daily schedule that morning, but we were all wondering what that could mean. Personally, I didn't like the sound of it. I have to deal with challenges all year long; I was hoping this mandatory vacation would at least mean some peace and quiet.

We had to split up into groups and complete five challenges.

CHALLENGES

1 "DISARMED"
2 "BLIND MAKEUP"
3 "IF YOU SING"
4 "TASTE TRACE"
5 "TILKINLIWITHI"

The good news is that I wound up on a team with Maxence, Clara, Mehdi, and Coline. We decided to start with the first challenge, "disarmed." One after another, we all had to act like we were brushing our teeth 😁 — except someone else was standing behind us using their arms instead! I was with Clara. . . . Man, she's pretty cute—OK, I know I said it already—and I have to admit that being on a team with her didn't bother me one bit. 🙂

But if you ask me, I don't think I'm going to charm the ladies by doing all these goofy activities. 😐

I quickly ended up with toothpaste all over my face, which sure made everyone else laugh. 😝 But even that was still better than Aldo's team—they were playing "taste trace." The goal of that one was to try different foods with a blindfold on. But I totally saw Aldo shove his finger up his nose and take out a green glob worthy of the *Guinness World Records* . . . before putting it in Quentin's mouth.

DISGUSTING! 😲

Quentin spit it all out and sprinted to the bathroom. Thankfully Samuel—the camp "elder"—avenged Quentin by making Aldo taste a scorching hot sauce. 😝 He nearly choked to death. He got all red, tears were streaming down his cheeks, and he yelled, "Mamma mia!" 😖 Then Samuel went to the leaders and told them Aldo was really upset, because he missed his parents and left his comfort blanket at home. We were literally rolling on the floor laughing. 😃 Aldo was blushing, and afterward he went and locked himself in his cabin. His team was automatically disqualified, but we continued the challenges without him.

Mamma mia!

For "blind makeup," ⊝ Killian was so slow he passed the time limit and none of his teammates got a chance to participate. For "if you sing," we had to sing a song while wearing headphones 🎧 that were playing a different one. But the girls cheated! We finished with "tilkinliwithi," where you have to replace all vowels in your sentences with the letter "i." (Get it? "Talk only with i.") It was hilarious. 😁 After it was all said and done, Gerald announced we were the winners!

Who are the champs of Champ Camp??

WE are!

They let us stay up thirty minutes later than everyone else and—get this—watch TV!

It's been almost FOUR DAYS since I last caught a glimpse of a screen, and believe me, I would've given anything to see one now . . .  even turned off! But after five minutes, none of us could keep our eyes open and we went off to bed.

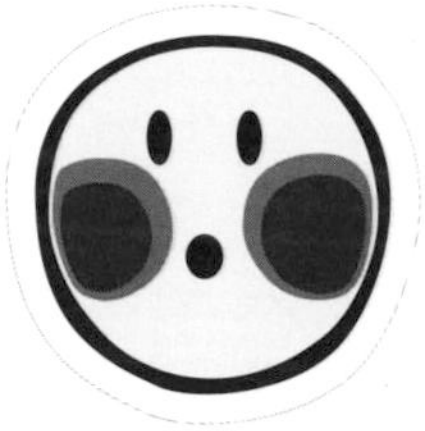

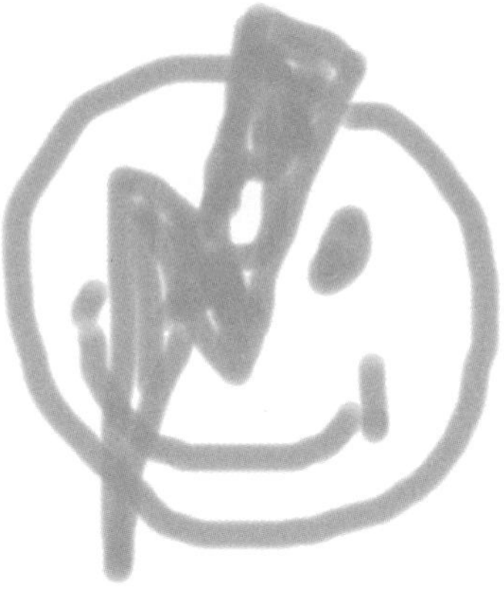

DAY 6
Thursday

Dear future
human,

Good news! First, I found the <u>key to my
journal</u>—it had slipped into my pillowcase.
Second, it's been two days since I've crossed
out my calendar, which means <u>time must be
passing FASTER</u>. I don't know what's gotten
into me, but Tuesday and Wednesday totally
flew by. A bit of candy, a dose of TV . . .
and here I am forgetting the best part:

COUNTING THE DAYS AND ABOVE ALL

PRETENDING

to join in on camp stuff. They're really good at
confusing you here. . . .

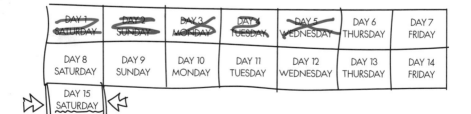

~~DAY 1 SATURDAY~~	~~DAY 2 SUNDAY~~	~~DAY 3 MONDAY~~	~~DAY 4 TUESDAY~~	~~DAY 5 WEDNESDAY~~	DAY 6 THURSDAY	DAY 7 FRIDAY
DAY 8 SATURDAY	DAY 9 SUNDAY	DAY 10 MONDAY	DAY 11 TUESDAY	DAY 12 WEDNESDAY	DAY 13 THURSDAY	DAY 14 FRIDAY
DAY 15 SATURDAY						

This morning, we woke up WAY earlier than usual because a fire alarm went off at 6:00 a.m.! It's strange—when we went out in the hallway, we found Aldo running back and forth yelling, "Al fuoco!" 🙂

Gerald and the counselors had to evacuate us calmly and quietly. I can confirm: it was a false alarm. 😮 But then we couldn't fall back asleep, so I took the opportunity to show my roommates the notebook I'd found underneath the bed. They seemed as surprised as I was, and Mehdi said we absolutely have to investigate. I wonder if it belongs to someone we know. . . . What if it was Pietro's? (Remember—my favorite soccer player?) Or what if it was a ghost's? 😬

Or what if it was YOU, future human, who went back in time and put it there to encourage me during this difficult time in my life? If that's it, take me back with you next time! Anyway, Yanis had a fantastic idea: he decided to call our secret meetings "the mystery council." Then Mehdi suggested we give everyone "code names." He said it made our mystery council "more secure" and . . . it was also cooler.

KIL   YAN   MAX   MEHD   MAX

Except there was one small problem with Maxence. . . .

Before we could figure out a solution, it was time for breakfast. I knew it was going to be a long day when I saw the dreadful mush that was waiting for us. 😕 Except for Romain—who got seconds—the tables were quickly covered with balled-up napkins full of disgusting rice pudding. And when Romain wanted to wipe his mouth, he accidentally picked up one of the napkins full of regurgitated mush. Yuk! 🤢

By the way, since the hike Tuesday, Fanny (one of the girls in our group) has been complaining of terrible eye pain. Naturally we all wanted to take a look at it. Aldo used this as an excuse to get close to her—and plant his lips right on hers! 😚 Fanny was furious, and Lola was . . . super jealous. Anyway, we haven't spotted anything in her eye.

pffff!

Girls: they're all sissies—except Naïs and Lena . . . and Célia, and I guess Clara too. And some people are ready to do whatever it takes to avoid camp.

The whole day was set aside for "horseback riding 101." Gerald had wanted to get some horses, but a group of tourists already reserved them all. So he had to make do <u>with ponies.</u> Believe me, at six feet tall, Samuel didn't exactly look dignified on top of his pony.

But guess what: The ponies didn't come alone. Dimitri, the instructor, bossed them around with a whip. I think it's safe to say that Yanis's anti-sun magic has stopped working.

Since I'm such a CHIVALROUS person, I let the girls go in front of me, 😎 then my friends, and then even Aldo. Valentin was right on my heels, and I got the sense that he didn't want this introduction to horseback riding any more than I did. Even though I promised to give him my waffle tomorrow morning, he wouldn't go in front of me.

Make no mistake, future human: my first lap was nothing to write home about. In fact, there was an enormous bush in the middle of the "ring." Dimitri helped me up onto my pony, and I was off. I started slowly to build my confidence. But after passing the bush, I found myself out of view of any adult who could possibly help me. That's when Comet, my pony (in my time, horses all have names like Star and Comet), started jerking, and all of a sudden I pitifully tipped over sideways.

It was impossible to straighten myself back up. I held onto the saddle as tightly as I could, but it took forever for Comet to come around the bush. I finally saw the group. Lou was staring at me, but because she's super timid, she didn't utter a single word. Aldo was also watching me . . . and making fun of me! But I guess I was OK with it this time, because at least he said something. Dimitri ran over to help me back up. A little more and it could have been a deadly fall! And if I was blushing, it was ONLY because my head was almost upside down, just to be clear!

I'll spare you the rest of the details from today. Once we got back to the cabin, I was just ready for it to be over. At least that's what I was hoping, but when it was time for showers, Aldo went and did it again. . . . He "disguised" himself as a girl and spoke in a high-pitched voice so he could get into the girls' showers.

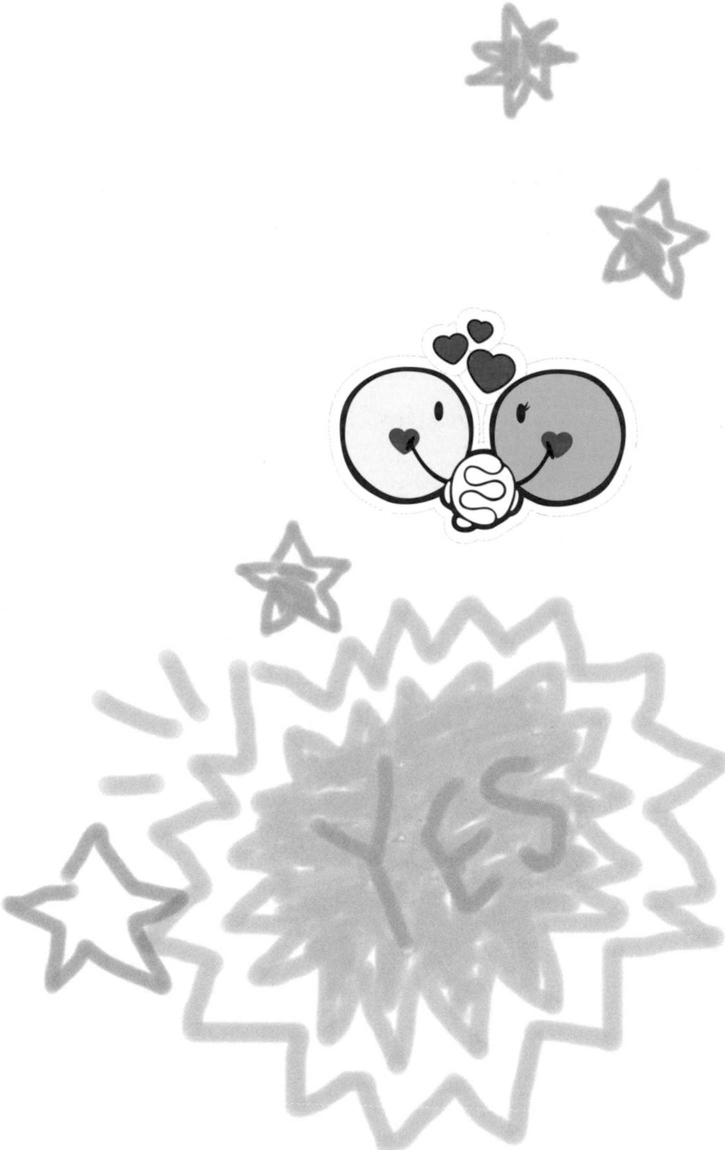
YES

DAY 7
Friday

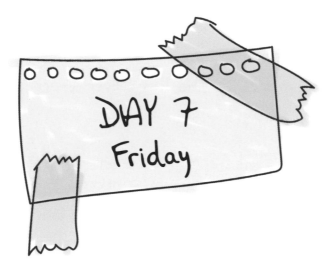

Dear future
       human,

The days just keep coming here, but at least
they're all different. Apparently, Anthony
played a joke on Caroline last night. He told
her that the girls were making a huge mess
in their rooms. So she went over there and
started yelling:

"That's enough already! Everyone needs
to go to sleep this instant, or else the
all-nighter tomorrow is cancelled!"

But actually, all the girls were already
sleeping—before Caroline woke them up, that
is! Hahaha!
  Something else crazy happened with Fanny.
Can you believe her eye was still hurting!
Caroline took a look at it yesterday morning
at breakfast, but she didn't see anything. So
Gerald sent her to the nurse's station, but
Rosette, the nurse, couldn't find anything either.

Then this morning when Fanny woke up, her eye was enormous—totally swollen. They immediately sent her to see a doctor, and it turns out she'd been stung by something and was having a severe allergic reaction. 😖

I remembered something unbelievable that I'd heard one time. Evidently there are bugs in the jungle that can lay eggs under people's skin. 😮 Eww, right??? It's horrible! Just telling you about it grosses me out. But after thinking about it, I kinda wished something like that would've happened to ME, because Gerald called Fanny's parents and they came to pick her up right away. Lucky!!! 🙂 Thankfully, this time they were smart enough to send the parents around to the back of her cabin, which prevented widespread mutiny.

But wait, that's
not all! I think
today must've been
national insect day
or something.
When Lou woke
up this morning,
she looked like she'd been
turned into a mosquito buffet.
She was covered with at least
fifty-three bites!

53 BUMPS

All you
can eat!

But the worst was Gabriel. The guy
just can't catch a break . . . he's one of
Aldo's roommates. And at one point last
night, he started screaming like a maniac
because there was a big brown worm
in his bed. When Anthony showed
up, Gabriel explained that he was sure he'd
caught a tapeworm, because his older brother
had already had one and he knew EXACTLY
what they looked like.

It's a good thing I didn't know about this little crisis when it was happening, but apparently Anthony was freaked out. He went to the dining hall to look for a jar, caught the worm with a pair of tweezers, and sealed it up tight in the container.

In the morning, Gabriel went to see the doctor along with Fanny, but the doctor only needed one look at the little guy in the jar to determine Gabriel's situation was actually MUCH less serious. The worm was in fact a mere earthworm . . . that Aldo had found very amusing to slide into his bed. 😁 All of this threw the camp into chaos, so much so that the morning activities were cancelled. No one in the dining hall was hungry—it totally ruined our appetites. The last day of this week wasn't looking very promising. ☹

Luckily, things took a turn for the better in the afternoon, during the much-awaited "mail delivery."

The leaders were sharing updates with our families, thanks to the Champ Camp blog. But since phones and electronics were banned, the camp set up "Friday mail." The idea was to write real paper letters to our families, like in the old days. And believe me, we really tried our best.

Dear Kitty,
meow
meow
meow
meow
meow
meow
meow.
—Lou

I love you guys, but I don't miss you at all.
—Salomé

Can I come home now?
—Q

Mom + Dad = Kiss + Love ♡

Dear Daddy, I miss you I hope you're still alive!
—C

Mom, Dad! I'm OK. I'm having fun. Good news: there's no class here. —G

Hey, miss you
—C

I smile in photos so you think it's going well, but it's really awful.
—V

They're forcing me to write to you! —S

ALDO, THE PRANKMASTER

I Need $50!!

Aldo!xx

Mom, Dad,
We eat well here:
pizzas, fries, waffles,
and fried
chicken. —R ☺

Gerald also passed out fill-in-the-blank letters, which I, for one, found very helpful and thorough.

Dear parents

Camp is meh!

Today Gabriel found a tapeworm in his bed.

I love counting the days and pretending to have fun.

The weather is horrible. This camp's a rip-off!

What I like most is nothing.

My roommates are smell bad and snore.

The leaders are really mean.

Send me Come get me!

I love you not.

PS: Just kidding!

Tonight Gerald and the counselors organized a "stargazing night hike" to celebrate the end of the first week. Most people were complaining because they'd been expecting a party. I, on the other hand, wasn't the slightest bit bothered. Dear future human, you remember how much I love the summer meteor shower in Brittany—and anything else remotely related to astronomy? This was a good opportunity to show off all the constellations I know . . . and was sure to impress the girls. Sure enough, all I had to do was utter the words "Ursa Major" and "Cassiopeia," and then Lola and Coline ~~fell into my arms~~ came up to me. But most importantly, Clara totally held hands with me!

In the dark of night, all kinds of things could have happened between us . . . 😊 if Aldo hadn't pushed Valentin in a "trace of life," as Gerald called it. . . .

trace of life= cow poop

That totally ruined the vibe between Clara and me! We had to go back to camp earlier than planned because Valentin was totally fed up. And that's how our last night before the new kids arrived went down the drain. 😞

You know, I almost forgot: starting tomorrow, it's no longer just us. And especially because Fanny left, we're going to be the MINORITY! We all agreed earlier to show them right away who the bosses here are.

In the meantime, Mehd, Max, Yan, Kil, and I held a meeting of our "mystery council" in our room. We pulled out the anonymous notebook. We turned it around every which way. . . . 😊 😊 😊 Nothing. Still nothing. I was about two seconds away from just throwing it in the trash when—I have no idea why—I lifted it up and held it to the ceiling light. You wouldn't have believed your eyes. The journal was covered in writing, scrawled in invisible ink!

DAY 8
Saturday

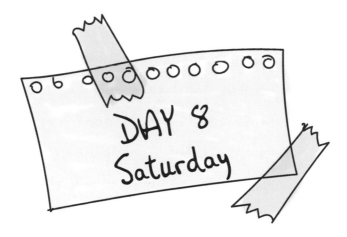

Dear future
human,

Last night's discovery totally threw everyone for a loop. But we still haven't been able to read what's written in the diary, because just after we noticed the writing, Anthony immediately called for lights out. 🙁 Seriously!

And then there's Clara: I don't really know where I stand. Everything happened a little too fast last night. Now because of my overactive imagination . . . or because of the pile of poop that "hindered" my romantic destiny, I'm wondering if I didn't just dream she held my hand, you know? 😳

I decided to choose ignorance and (PRETEND) nothing happened. We'll see where that leads. Especially because this whole situation runs the risk of making me feel guilty about Naïs.

Anyway, today even more crazy stuff happened to me . . . at least something that I wasn't expecting at all. Even you won't be able to get over it! Once again, my life is full of unexpected developments, and all of the records I'm leaving for the future FOR FREE won't be in vain! You'll see!

This morning, the leaders started the day by reading some of the messages left by parents on the Champ Camp blog. Believe me, some were absolutely priceless.

Hi there my little Gabypoo, I check the Champ Camp blog every day. Your little sister cries all the time because she misses you so much. If only we could have slid into your suitcase! ;) Mommy

Sweetheart,
Every day, you fill us with joy.
Your smile is like fresh air.
You'll always be in our hearts.
We love our little dove from above!
Daddy

How embarrassing!

To our darling,
I just wanted to say you make our lives full.
Angel, we love you times in-finity!
Your parents.
PS: Don't stay up too late, and we hope you have the sweetest of dreams.

Ouch!

Hey sweet princess,
You seem so well-behaved in
your photos. We're proud of
you. Come back happy, having
shared these special moments.
We can't wait for you to come
home.
Big kisses,
Mom and Dad
PS: Don't forget to brush
your teeth.

The humiliation!

Time for the hoodie tactic

Valy, our prince,
So how's camp? We're
already thinking about the
day you get back, when we
can have a little mara-
thon with you and hear all
about your stay.
Mimi and Pawpaw

To our dearest Nathan,
Make sure to wear your
scarf and hat when you go
out and the weather's not
nice—you'll be fine!!
Your parents, who love you
to the moon and back

My Loulou!
Thanks Champ Camp for the beautiful pictures! You look like a little prince in your friend's checkered T-shirt. This weekend is gloomy without you; thankfully, the sun came back out. . . .
Mom

LOL

Good evening, adventurers,
Heya Roro,
We hope that everything's going well, that you're eating well, and that you love the wood-fired pizzas. We'll make them again at home. We saw the photos—you have the right to wear your own pajamas!!! ;)
Hugs and kisses from Dad, Mom, and Spike.

How precious

We all received mail. Even me. I opened the letter from my mom first. She must have sent it last Thursday, judging from the post office stamp.

Even so, I thought she could've written me earlier. But when I opened the envelope, about twenty paper-cutout red lipstick prints flew in my face.

I scrambled to gather them all before the others noticed. Then I opened a card from . . . umm . . . uhh . . . a certain person . . . umm . . . umm . . . who I won't mention by name:

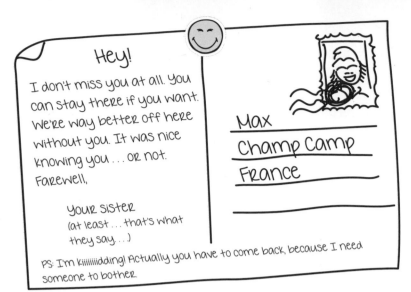

Hey!

I don't miss you at all. You can stay there if you want. We're way better off here without you. It was nice knowing you ... or not. Farewell,

Your sister
(at least ... that's what they say ...)

PS: I'm kiiiiiiiidding! Actually you have to come back, because I need someone to bother.

Max
Champ Camp
France

Marion is so annoyyyyyyng!

Aldo tried to snatch the letter Valentin got from his parents out of his hand. Fortunately, the counselors spotted him and sent him to the cabin to write, "I must respect the privacy of others" one hundred times. 😁

I also had a little postcard from Grandpa Joff and Grandma Ragny in my mail, which said they couldn't wait for me to visit. I'm really excited to tell them all about my adventures.

But above all, there was a letter from Tom and Nico. These two slugs mentioned Nico's mom had printed some more IAG stuff. They also went by Pleasant Gardens just after I left. Nico had the brilliant idea 🍼 to bring up our fundraiser with the community center, and Hugo, the supervisor, found a time slot for them to organize a booth to sell more items for Welcoming Wheelchairs. Tom said that everything was going well with Célia. Apparently she might be the one! As for Nico, he's been spending a lot of time at Léna's 💚 house—who, by the way, adopted her service doggy Babouk. Tom said he was leaving soon for his grandparents' house in the Basque country, like every year. That means I won't see him again before school starts in September. 😟 Nico was more vague. From what I understand, he's going out of town but didn't really specify where. With a little luck, we'll be able to hang out the last week of July.

Even if I have to admit that life here is less awful than I'd imagined, I still feel a little jealous knowing they're all together and I'm . . . EXILED, miles away, unable to escape from this dump! All the more because at the end of the letter, they said they had something SUPER IMPORTANT to tell me about Naïs. These two clowns didn't want to say anything more about it. Result:

it started messing with my head.

Next, I went with Mehdi to see the new weekly program that Gerald had put up on the announcement board. Tonight there's a special "welcome cookout" for the new campers. No worries—we're ready to show them we're the stronger ones! But then we noticed something that Yanis couldn't, under any circumstances, find out about.

WEDNESDAY   THURSDAY

WILDERNESS TREK

If he sees this, he's going to chant even more spells in his sleep and we're not going to get a minute of shut-eye. Even worse, the weather is supposed to be "glorious" all week. So there's NO WAY the activity will be cancelled.

We wondered if we would have to skin rabbits, drink our own pee, or eat snails and grasshoppers and all that. <u>TWO DAYS IN THE WOODS?</u> This was looking bad, but at least I already have some basic adventurer knowledge, thanks to Tom.

After that we played a little soccer 🙂⚽ tournament, and in the afternoon it was time for "Cook Nook!" 👨‍🍳—a cooking workshop. Aldo seized at another opportunity to complain and said, "Cooking eez a thing for-a geerls," and that he'd rather play more soccer. But the class was actually kind of fun; Caroline and Anthony suggested we make dessert for dinner tonight: chocolate candy! 🙂 Max, Mehd, Yan, Kil, and I all thought the idea was pretty good. Especially when Clara asked if I wanted to work together with her. It seems like there's a good chance I really didn't dream: Clara is head over heels for me. I guess I'm just a bona fide chick magnet. OK, fine, I'll admit I may have a certain natural charisma, but it's really not that easy for me. You know, dear future human, all this doesn't really jive with the whole Naïs thing. I love her, and we've got something steady going on. 🙂

You know me: I'm an honest guy, the kind of guy who's sure of himself! So I stuck to my supremely tricky technique, the stealth mode I alone had mastered: PRETENDING I couldn't care less!

On another note, it's crazy how what we made didn't end up looking AT ALL like what the leaders did! I've got to say, my finished dessert looked way more like the turds from Rocky, my neighbor Miss Roudan's dog, than a chocolate candy.

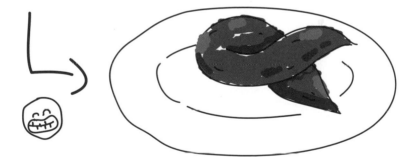

At the time, I wasn't so sure the newcomers would appreciate this kind of welcome. But in the end, I figured it might chase them away a little faster.

They showed up around seven! Our group was a total mess. The counselors had told us to gather outside and welcome them with the camp song. But Valentin was way too timid to handle something so nerve-racking, so he went to hide in his room. And Aldo did some kind of ridiculous Aztec dance around their bus. 😁 The new guys got off the bus, and there was a crazy scramble for everyone to find their bags. All of the chaos prevented me from getting a really good look at any of them. A few minutes later, I suddenly felt a strange presence behind me.

At first I thought it was Aldo, so when I turned around, I almost jumped down his throat. But who was it? You'll never believe it! Nicolas Frilo!

NICO! MY BUDDY!

Unbelievable, right? I almost exploded with joy. Good luck was finally smiling upon me! And believe me, I wasn't the only one happy to see a familiar face. We gave each other a huge hug. . . . I mean, we patted each other on the back . . . you know, like real men!

I introduced him to my friends right away: Mehdi, Maxence, Yanis, and the whole gang. Nico told me later that, when he found out I'd gone to camp, he begged his mom to sign him up too. He said he was as bored as a goldfish in a bowl, all alone at home, after Tom and Léna went on vacation.

And luckily, there was still one spot left for this week. Our lucky break! 🙂 My camp friends and I gave him a tour of the place and helped him unpack. I would've liked for him to join our room, but his group is in the other building, closer to the girls' cabin. And since I get along really well with Mehdi and the others, I wasn't going to betray them by asking to switch rooms.

From now on, there are more leaders: Manon, Élisa, and Kader. They're the ones who called everyone over for the cookout. And I've got to admit—we all had a great night! 😃

To give you an idea of what the place is like: the whole property is surrounded by a forest, and right in the middle there's a little clearing with a fire pit. We all gathered around the fire.

The newcomers introduced themselves, thanks to the talking stick, and then we sang the camp anthem again under the stars.

The leaders grilled fish. Romain gulped down second and third helpings, so fast that he lodged a fishbone on the roof of his mouth.

FISHBONE

As for me, I'm pretty sure this little feast brought me around to the idea of eating fish, which I normally hate. Then Aldo and Samuel were selected to pass out the chocolate candy we'd made this afternoon. Around the fire, everyone burst into laughter when they saw what the dessert looked like, but it was actually pretty good.

Afterward, Mehdi and I told Nico about our discovery of the secret anonymous notebook, and we officially "inducted" him into our mystery council. On the other side of the campfire, I caught Clara's eye, but she immediately looked away. She seemed sad.

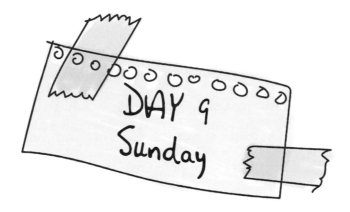

DAY 9
Sunday

Dear future
human,

I'll spare you the details of this awful day,
which was mostly set aside for . . . <u>a medieval</u>
<u>tournament.</u>

It was our group against the new kids. On
the agenda: archery, orienteering, and jousting—
during which, instead of being a knight, I
ended up as Aldo's squire. . . . To be honest,
he didn't look very impressive on top of his
steed.

It reminded me of
the stupid postcard of
Raoul Kador at a rodeo last year,
after he got back from Texas.

Then it was laundry time, which wasn't exactly <u>delightful</u>. I think if my parents had shown up at camp, they'd have been forced to wear a gas mask. Quite a few of us have given up on showering. The girls took forever in the laundry room, so when it was finally our turn, there wasn't any water left.

Dylan and Hugo went to go complain to Gerald, who was in the middle of watering the plants.

We followed them, but we really shouldn't have: the response was drastic, worthy of "real men," according to the director.

The whole evening was devoted to an event in the activity room: *The Mehdi Show.* This dork volunteered to "perform" in front of the whole camp. Gerald, no doubt a little short on ideas after all these years, accepted his offer without a second's hesitation! After we'd moved all the chairs from the dining hall for the show, I ran into Mehdi "backstage." He had a serious case of stage fright.

His reaction was totally normal, and I could relate: Last year I was pretty nervous at Pleasant Gardens, when I had to sing "Hope and Life." So I gave him a little pep talk and a few relaxation tips I stole from *Children Soft as Pandas* 🐼 —without saying where I got them, of course. Mainly I just told him, based on my own experience, "Don't think, just go for it! You've got this!"

In the audience, I wound up sitting between Nico and Clara. 😉 I suspect my buddy set that one up. Which reminds me: when Nico arrived last night, I immediately asked him about Naïs. Guess what . . . he and Tom bumped into her a few times, hand in hand with some older dude—maybe sixteen years old. Neither one of them knew who the guy was, but Naïs and this loser seemed to be getting along a little too well. If I see him when I get back, he's gonna be in for a rough time, I guarantee it!

Me

Naïs's moron

This news totally shocked me, and it's undoubtedly the reason I was off my game during the medieval tournament that morning. If I had to sum up my current romantic situation in one word, it'd be: heartbroken! 🙁 And believe me, it really hurts for Maxime Cropin the Great to admit something like that. I'm definitely going to have to set things straight when school starts. But I'm already wondering how I'll be able to do that, because even though I'm a chick magnet, I don't know much about love yet. 🙂

The lights dimmed, the velvet curtain parted, and Mehdi appeared on the stage. For a good half hour, he told every joke he had and managed to really get the crowd going.

During the performance, I got the feeling that Clara was waiting for me to make a move. The tension between us was "electric," but . . . I was still in stealth mode. Eventually Nico elbowed me and gave me a look that said, "What are you waiting for?!"

Jeez! I'm taking my time, man! You can't rush me. I'm already in a state of shock about my near break-up with Naïs, as I see it. I need TIME.

We all got up to applaud for Mehdi. Lola, Mélissa, Paloma, and Cassandre even went and asked him for an autograph . . . which made me a tiny bit jealous. Then it was curfew time, so we all went back to our rooms.

But Mehdi and I didn't plan on going to bed right away. . . . Killian, on the other hand, crashed the minute the lights went out. Maxence and Yanis preferred to keep a lookout.

We waited for almost an hour for everything to quiet down: Yanis went out into the hallway to make sure that everyone else was sleeping and that the counselors had also gone off to bed. I took the anonymous journal, and Mehdi and I tiptoed back to the activity room where we'd planned to rendezvous with Nico.

But Nico wasn't alone. He and Arthur were there waiting for us. Arthur is one of Nico's roommates, and to be honest, I wasn't too happy at first to have an outsider tag along. But since it was dark and turning on a light would've been way too risky, Arthur offered to go look for candles in the kitchen.

It was perfect timing, because we'd also celebrated Coline's birthday this afternoon. In the end I figured this guy was actually pretty cool, especially when he came back with not only a bag of candles but also an enormous chocolate pound cake he'd found in a cupboard. 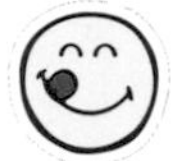

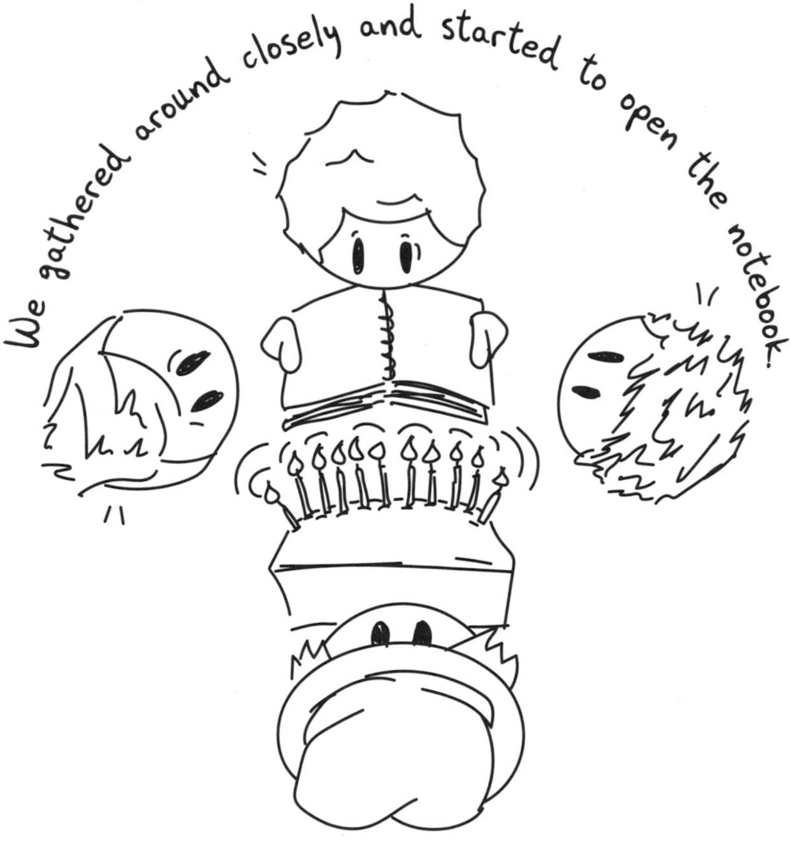
We gathered around closely and started to open the notebook.

It was almost time to reveal the mystery!
And make no mistake—thanks to *The
Resourceful Ranger's Handbook*, I knew exactly
how to analyze invisible ink. All I had to do
was heat the first page using the candle to
discover the initial letters:

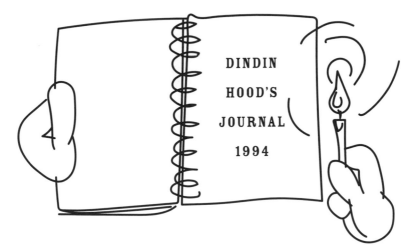

DINDIN

HOOD'S

JOURNAL

1994

I don't know how much time we spent
reading the journal, dear future human, but
it turns out by some strange coincidence that
the author—this notorious Dindin Hood—starts
each of his pages in the exact same way I do:
by addressing the human of the future. It's
incredible, right?

He talks about plenty of stuff we've already experienced here: the fish cookouts, the talking stick, a certain Claire stuck in the bathroom. He even mentions a young counselor, Gerald! But above all, this notebook, written over twenty years ago, is in fact . . .

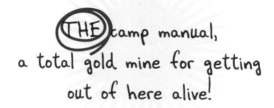

THE camp manual,
a total gold mine for getting
out of here alive!

It's a unique, visionary account of the last century. It's brimming with all kinds of tricks, such as:

☐ how to tie knots,

☐ filter water with a sock,

and even · · ·

☐ how to flirt with girls:

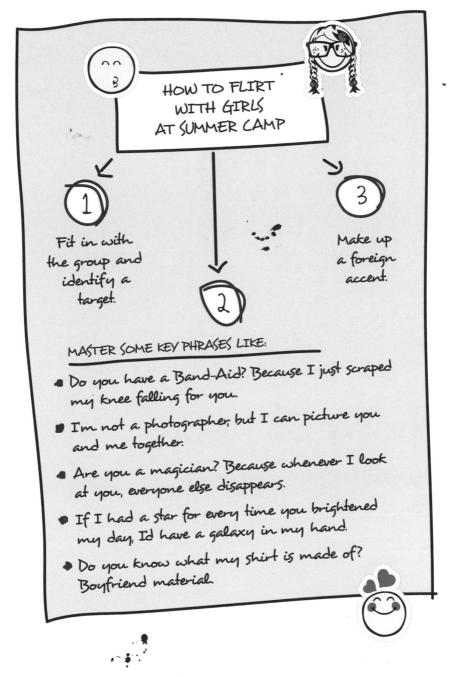

HOW TO FLIRT
WITH GIRLS
AT SUMMER CAMP

1 Fit in with the group and identify a target.

2 MASTER SOME KEY PHRASES LIKE:

- Do you have a Band-Aid? Because I just scraped my knee falling for you.
- I'm not a photographer, but I can picture you and me together.
- Are you a magician? Because whenever I look at you, everyone else disappears.
- If I had a star for every time you brightened my day, I'd have a galaxy in my hand.
- Do you know what my shirt is made of? Boyfriend material.

3 Make up a foreign accent.

A godsend, an absolute treasure, I guarantee it! And with only five days left at camp, it's about time something like this fell into my lap.

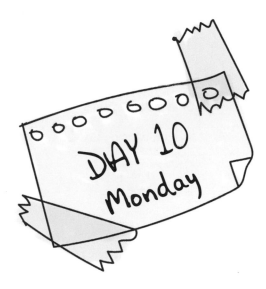

DAY 10
Monday

Today at Champ Camp was honestly not that great. Killian, Hugo, and Maeva found out they have lice. So that meant we all had to go through the treatment. Then Lola and Salomé got in a fight because of something having to do with clothes. . . . Anyway, the mood throughout the camp was tense, until I received 100% confirmation that Clara has a crush on me.

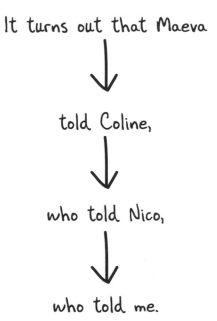

It turns out that Maeva

↓

told Coline,

↓

who told Nico,

↓

who told me.

I thought about it for a bit and decided I'm WAY too young to stay single. I decided to move from stealth mode to attack mode!

But like I already told you, things aren't that simple.

You won't believe it, but last night, when we were in the activity room carrying out our investigation, Clara, Coline, Lola, Salomé, and some other girls snuck out to our building.

Back in my room Killian was sleeping, but Yanis and Maxence wanted to mess with us by switching beds while we were gone.  Maxence was in my bed when Clara showed up. She said something like:

"Max, are you there?"

"Yeah," Maxence said. "Over here, the bottom bunk on the right."

"Max, umm . . . how should I say this . . . do you want to go out with me?"

"Uhh . . . yeah, OK."

smack! *smack!*

And that little weasel took advantage of the confusion between our similar names (which had been common knowledge at camp for a few days) to kiss her!

It's true! I swear!

Needless to say, she realized it the second she heard Yanis bust out laughing. She turned on the light, and, according to what they told me, bolted out the door. It's lucky that the leaders didn't wake up. Luckier still that Maxence didn't think about touching my secret pillow!

And this morning at breakfast, Clara had disappeared. I decided to take things into my own hands. I scribbled a note on a piece of paper and passed it to Sarah, who went to give it to Clara in the nurse's office—where she'd apparently decided to quarantine herself for the rest of the week.

The [offensive] method worked like a charm: Sarah delivered the note for me, Clara checked the YES box with a heart, and then Clara came back herself about an hour later. Her eyes were all red, but she had a big smile. 😍

Tonight, we snuck back out to the activity room again, and believe me—Maxence and Yanis better not even so much as look at my bed!

Using candlelight, we continued reading *Dindin Hood's Journal* to pick up as many pointers as possible before the wilderness trek taking place in less than forty-eight hours.

But the craziest part of this story is that Dindin Hood seemed to have exactly the same outlook on life as me . . . albeit less recent. He wasn't afraid of being an astronaut lost in space, but he talked constantly about his phobia of the Bermuda Triangle. He was obsessed with Explosix candy and thought that we'd all be living in wind turbines in twenty years. You'd have thought he was my clone or something. . . . It scared the crap out of me!

We sat around trying to figure out who this guy could really be. That's when Nico came up with the idea of the century: make a little trip to Gerald's office. We looked through all his cabinets and found a file from 1994 with all the health records for everyone at Champ Camp that year. And we found a form for our anonymous author.

Believe it or not, but this notorious Charles Dindin ALSO turned out to be my exact doppelganger from the past! OK, perhaps slightly less "charismatic," if you want my opinion. Let's not push it! Just then, we heard something in the hallway and rushed to hide.

It was Gerald, who was doing his night rounds. I held my breath . . . and phew! He left. We practically sprinted back to our rooms, but the recent discovery kept me awake for another hour. Maybe time is nothing but an eternal cycle, and there's another Max Cropin out there somewhere, in his forties.

Oh yeah, by the way, I sat next to Clara during the outdoor movie tonight. We gazed at each other—and even smiled! I'm pretty good, aren't I? I think I'm becoming a man.

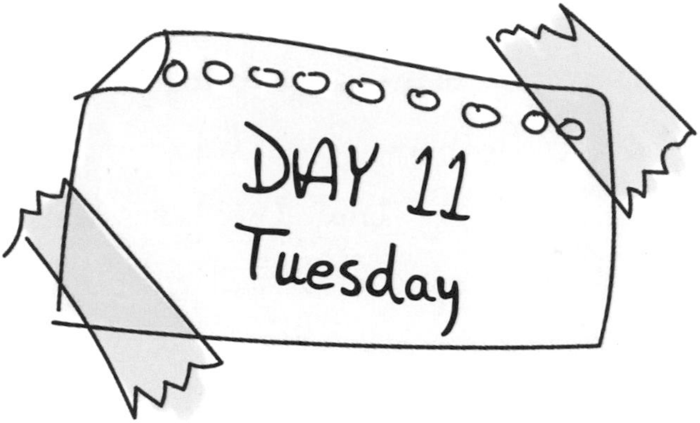
DAY 11
Tuesday

Dear future  human,

We spent most of the day preparing for our "survival outing" tomorrow: packing all our things into our backpacks . . . which proved to be much more difficult for the girls. For example, Lola wanted to bring her travel hairdryer. Anthony regretfully informed her that the trees didn't have electrical outlets installed yet. We gathered canteens, compasses, ponchos, first-aid kits, and food. We also made a mascot, a kind of totem pole that Nico and I thought up.

Next Gerald, like a seasoned adventurer, rallied us in the activity room to teach us some survival "basics." He went over how to find food and water in the woods, how to use a fire starter, and how to recognize certain edible fruits 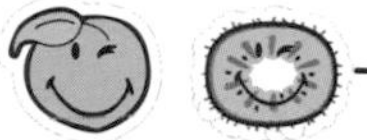—all the while emphasizing the "importance of staying together." Then he reminded us of his famous "rule of four threes."

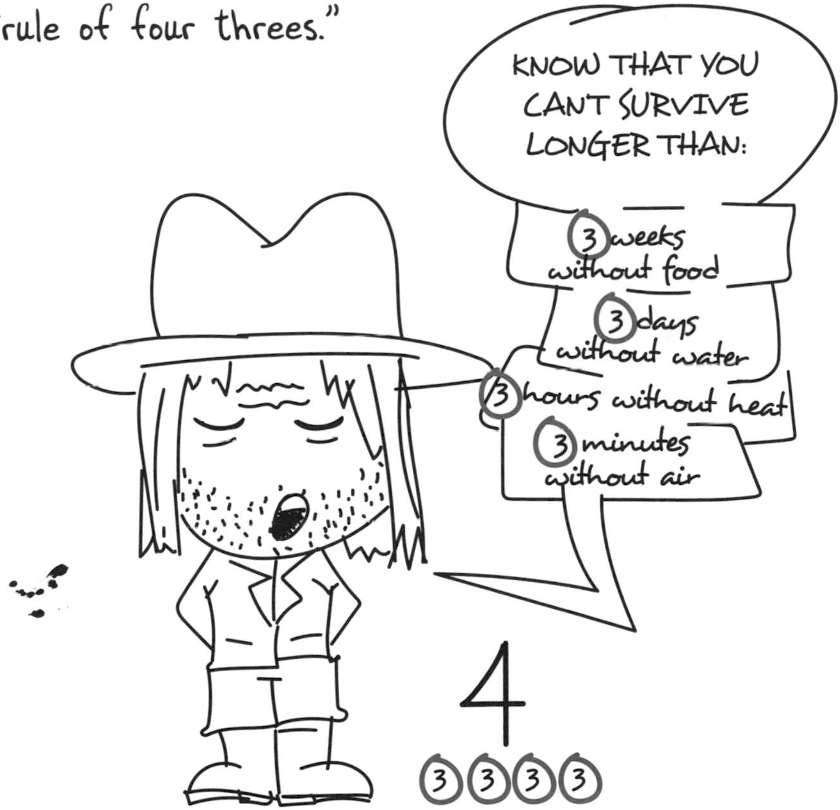
KNOW THAT YOU CAN'T SURVIVE LONGER THAN:
3 weeks without food
3 days without water
3 hours without heat
3 minutes without air
4
3 3 3 3

Mehdi, Nico, Arthur, and I already knew the rules because we'd read them word for word in Dindin's notebook. But the rest of the group was shaking in their boots. That's when Aldo broke the ice and asked:

And how-a long can a boy-a survive weethout-a geerls?

Dear future human, I leave tomorrow. I don't know if I'll make it out of this adventure in one piece,  so just in case, I'd like to say farewell. . . . Like Marion would say, it was nice knowing you. . . .

 SHE'S SO ANNOYYYYYING!

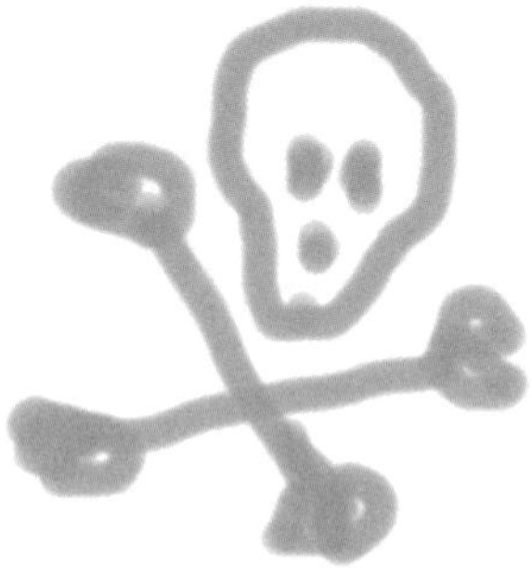

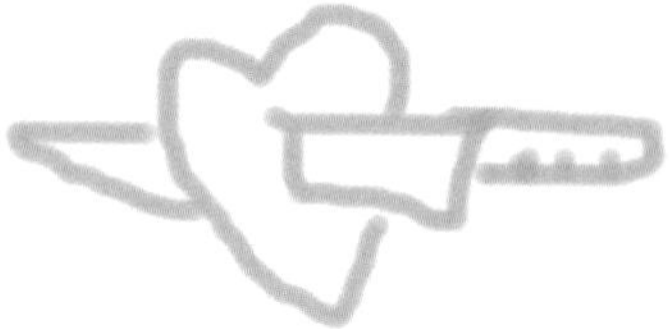

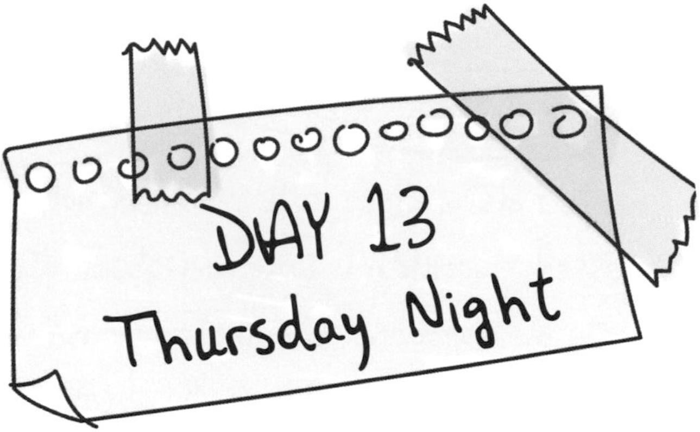
DAY 13
Thursday Night

Dear future  human,

At the time of writing this to you, I've just returned from the "wilderness trek," and I have good news:

I'M STILL ALIVE!

Well . . . it was a close call. . . . As you probably guessed, I couldn't take my observation notebook with me, because the instructions were clear: bring as little as possible, only absolute necessities to avoid weighing down our packs. We left yesterday morning at dawn. As expected, Yanis had spent the whole night reciting incantations, and he was dragging his feet from the get-go. And Killian was running on autopilot, still fully asleep.

Keep moving, Killian!

Oh c'mon, I'm going as fast as I can!

No one really knew what to expect. There was nothing but radio silence from the counselors. None of them wanted to tell us what we were going to do. But then we saw that all five of them were dressed in camouflage, which put us all on edge. We just imagined <u>all the unthinkable</u> things they had in store.

Even though the leaders encouraged us to "keep up our team spirit," we hiked for hours with all of these dark thoughts on our minds. 😫 And believe me—the hike last week was nothing compared to what was waiting for us.

I think I even saw Aldo dropping bread crumbs behind him.

(First:) he was wasting food.

(Second:) he must not have read the right version of *Hansel and Gretel*, which clearly shows the pebble option is better than breadcrumbs.

The farther we went, the deeper we sank into the woods. The dampness chilled our bones, and the darkness grew heavier and heavier. It was totally <u>freaky</u>!

But after a while, we finally stopped. Gerald and the counselors announced that we'd arrived at our "base camp" for the next two days. An "ideal" spot, near a river, sheltered by enormous trees. Mehdi, Nico, Yanis, the others, and I FAILED TO SEE exactly what was "ideal" about the situation or exactly how we'd survive in the middle of nowhere. There wasn't a cell phone tower in sight, in case we needed to call someone in an emergency, but Gerald and the counselors seemed to know the drill.

Then we all got together and the director gave us this whole speech about "determination," "cooperation," and all sorts of other words with "tion" that didn't mean anything fun.

They told us the first thing to do in a "critical" situation was to start making a shelter. I looked all around and then elbowed Mehdi and Nico: not the slightest trace of a hut or cabin in the area. That's when I realized they were going to make us <u>build our own!</u> 🙁

The girls' patrol immediately set off to look for twigs and leaves to start a pile. The boys' patrol had to find branches big enough to be the base of the structure for two shelters—one for girls and one for guys. And that's

when Valentin came hurtling with his arms full of mushrooms, hollering to everyone that he'd found food and we were saved thanks to him.

←

He was just about to put one in his mouth when we heard a shout.

Gerald stepped in just in time. Valentin was about to poison himself with a toxic mushroom, which earned us another long speech on all of the various risks of eating mushrooms found in the forest.

After the sudden adrenaline rush that almost knocked us all out, we got back to work. But even though I tried to remember the advice written in *Dindin Hood's Journal*, it took us a while to build our shelters under the leaders' "strict" supervision. Let's just say we were fighting for our lives. But in the end, looking at our two shelters, you could easily tell that the boys' was the <u>winner</u>.

Unfortunately, we celebrated a little too soon. Five minutes later, our "lean-to" collapsed on top of Samuel, who'd sat down inside of it and then leapt to his feet too quickly. Samuel probably should've had his own "private" shelter, given he's practically a giant. Anyway, his popularity among the guys plummeted. The girls got a good laugh out of the whole thing, and then we had to start all over.

Next, Gerald told us that the second step was to make a fire to dry the ground, repel insects, and above all . . . scare off animals. We didn't find this all too reassuring, to be honest.

So he showed us how to light a fire with moss, twigs, and all kinds of other things Tom and I had never managed to figure out. Aldo volunteered to blow on the coals, but right when the first sparks appeared, our only hope of survival went up in smoke! 😣

Gerald ended up pulling a lighter and some fire starters out of his pocket, which proved to be MUCH more effective.

The leaders then said it was time to eat. Everyone cheered. Believe me, future human, we meant it. We were all hoping that they had some fresh sandwiches or juicy hamburgers stashed away in their packs. But once again:

DISAPPOINTMENT!

They only had packets full of some weird substance: at first glance, it looked like a blend of vomit and dog food. But whatever it was, once it was mixed with some boiled river water, it actually wasn't too bad. And for that matter, I figured I should get used to this kind of food since it's probably what astronauts eat.

Dear future human, do you only eat packets of powder? If so, that's kind of annoying, because I love my mom's steak-and-potato Sunday dinners. I don't know how I'll live without them in the future. . . .

Anyway, the real problem was that, after gulping this sketchy mush down, we were all still <u>super hungry.</u> That's when Manon, Élisa, and Kader—the counselors from Nico's group—pulled out a bag of cake flour. It was a little something to "boost our morale," they explained.

We went back into the woods to look for little branches. But it was pitch black, and even with our flashlights we could barely see a few feet in front of us.

At one point, Samuel started crying out

OOOOOOWHOOOOOOO!

to make us think there were wolves. I really thought that Valentin, even at the ripe old age of thirteen, was going to pee his pants. We got back to camp with some good sticks, wrapped little balls of dough around the end, and held our skewers over the fire.

It was delicious! Have you ever had freshly baked bread before, dear future human? There's nothing better! OK, one thing would've made it better—chocolate icing!

We sang Champ Camp's song, then the leaders went off on their own so we'd have some time to ourselves. Not a moment too soon, if you ask me! The discussion quickly turned to the going-away party on Friday night, boys and girls, and rumors about who likes who.

That's when Aldo came up with a fantastic idea: everyone would <u>secretly</u> write down the names of people they thought should date. Since we didn't have any paper or pencils, we took some leaves and poked our sticks into the coals. Then, one by one, we dropped our leaves into one of Aldo's shoes. He shook it up, and, as you can probably imagine, half of them were erased. But some were still intact.

I think some people just made up crushes,
because I'd never noticed Mehdi eying Mélissa
or Nico ogling at Coline. But it was obvious
that Clara not only wanted to go out with me,
but also my roommate Maxence wanted to go
out with her, ever since the mix-up in our room.
I'm betting it's gonna be a real mess.

Right after we finished reading the leaves, the leaders whistled for curfew and we went off to bed. We were so exhausted, we didn't fight it. The ONLY thing we wanted was peace and quiet, but ohhhhh no!

Around one in the morning, I heard Anthony bringing Valentin back to our campsite. Valentin was so afraid of sleeping out in the open that he'd tried to sneak off. But he barely got twenty feet before he had to call out for help.

Once everything quieted back down, I heard something that sounded like plastic being rummaged through: it was Romain, who'd come down with a case of the munchies and woken up to look for a little snack to raid. After he went back to bed, he started snoring. We were squeezed together in our humble shelter like packaged hotdogs, and it was freezing cold. I had a heck of a time closing my eyes, and it was the same for Nico, Mehdi, and Yanis.

Right when we were finally about to fall asleep, I sat up and my heart started beating furiously: in the middle of the deathly quiet of the dark, black night, I heard footsteps outside! The fear! I whispered to Nico and Mehdi, telling them to be quiet and listen. I wasn't dreaming. An animal, surely wild and horrifying, was about to pounce on our lean-to and swallow us whole! We were going to suffer a horrible death, far from our families, abandoned to fate! Suddenly, we saw a ray of light approach, and a shadowy silhouette appeared at the entrance of our shelter. Nico, Mehdi, Yanis, and I were still so scared that we stuck together like glue. Then we recognized Lola's face, and then Mélissa's, then Coline's, and finally Clara's.

The girls all entered our shelter and explained that they hadn't managed to doze off, either. Basically, they asked if they could STAY WITH US! That's when Aldo, who we thought was sleeping, popped his head up:

But of-a course, geerls! The Prince of-a Love weelcomes you weeth-a open arms!

Well, the girls had already predicted this and brought their own blankets. They stuck to us like glue, and that's how I found myself lying down, in the middle of the night, deep in the woods, NEXT TO CLARA! I felt just as clumsy as when Naïs kissed me. . . . It was hardly a few weeks ago. . . .

It felt so distant. I wondered what was going to happen, when I heard her whisper something in my ear that blew me away: "Good night, Max."

Boom!

(First,) that tickled my eardrum, because I'm SUPER ticklish.

(Second,) I realized she wasn't in attack mode at all, but closer to stealth mode. Since I felt guilty about the Naïs situation, I didn't move a muscle. Then, I don't know how, but we all fell asleep really fast. It was a grueling day, all right?

The next day, the leaders woke us up at seven in the morning. (☹) They were not too happy to find the girls in our shelter, and they split us up ASAP. In order to "reprimand" us, and also to wake us up, we had the privilege of undergoing a military-style workout.

171

We had to do jumping jacks, thirty push-ups, and then run ten laps around our base camp. Believe me, on a scale of 1 to 10, I can say Mr. Ramoupoulos's PE class is a −3 compared to what we had to do! 😖 But—not for the faint-hearted—even worse trials were waiting for us. 😣 If we'd known ahead of time, I'm sure we would've rebelled against the camp leadership! But by the time we were out in the middle of nowhere, it was too late—we needed the counselors to guide us back to civilization. And this time around, there was no way I could PRETEND to have fun or get out of it.

By the way, I wish this whole expedition could've been filmed for TV or something like that. Our achievements, mine in particular, could've finally been revealed to the world . . . or at least a captive audience.

😉

Gerald and the counselors gathered everyone and gave us a pep talk that sent shivers down my spine.

Never give up! Give it everything you've got!

Easier said than done . . . especially after a night like the one we'd just experienced and the breakfast we had to choke down: cold leftover <u>kebabs</u> and sketchy <u>mush.</u> After breakfast, the leaders took us deep into the woods for what they called a "backwoods challenge." The goal?

Reconnect with nature, like our primitive ancestors.

Everyone had to first cover themselves in dirt and mud to blend in with the forest, then one team would hide within an area marked by bandanas tied to trees. The second team had to find everyone else. Even after the workout we'd just gone through, we were feeling OK and the idea of smearing ourselves with mud and leaves sounded pretty fun.

I was on a team with Nico, and I have to say, we had a ton of fun. And as luck would have it, none of us were found!

At the end of this escapade, Gerald and the counselors announced that we were going to fish 🐟 for our lunch before going back to camp. They taught us plenty of techniques to catch fish without equipment, like using branches to make a pole, making a fishing line out of clothing thread, or fashioning hooks and lures with little bones, wood, or even a nail. I made a mental note to tell Grandpa Joff about all of this next month—he loves fishing! 🕶️

Then, we gathered at the edge of the river and wound up catching five enormous fish that we cooked over a fire. You can bet we ate every last bite! To be honest, I was pretty proud of us. The "survival stage" was nearing its end, and we got through it just fine. We packed up our stuff—which didn't take long, given the fact that we hardly had anything—and lined up behind Gerald to follow the trail back.

But there was one last test. 🙁
Really, I swear!

After about an hour of hiking, Gerald and the counselors stopped the group. They explained that one of us was going to be given a compass and would be in charge of leading the group back to the "extraction point." By that, they meant back to Champ Camp. We drew straws, and guess who picked the shortest one? Yep . . . ME!

The fear of being an astronaut floating into nothingness started to creep up on me. I would've given just about anything to avoid taking on this responsibility. Nico and the others must've noticed the strange look on my face, because they surrounded me and started chanting words of encouragement.

Surrounded by tall trees, the echo of their cheering resonated throughout the forest. Under normal circumstances, I would've taken this as a sign that my genius was at last being recognized and my time to shine had finally come, but I wasn't really feeling too confident. I didn't have any other choice but to accept the mission. I took the compass, turned south, and signaled for the group to follow me.

But at one point, right when I was thinking camp couldn't be much farther, we came to the edge of a <u>huge ravine.</u> I stopped in my tracks, racking my brain for how we were going to get across. Then Gerald suggested I look up. I noticed a pulley and a harness, and then it hit me: we had to cross the ravine <u>by cable.</u>

Thankfully, the leaders didn't expect me to figure it out on my own. It was all part of the survival experience, but they hadn't given us any warning. All of a sudden, I heard a weird noise behind me.

CLACK CLACK CLACK CLACK ?

As for me, I was starting to really regret passing on Tom's invitations to do a high ropes course with him. But in light of my very recent surge in popularity and the encouragement Nico was sending from the corner of his eye, backing down was <u>out of the question!</u> Anyway, Anthony and Kader were the first to go over, so they could catch us on the other side.

Next it was my turn, since I'd been mercilessly appointed team leader. Gerald and Élisa helped me put on the harness. I sat down beneath the cable, grabbed the pulley with both hands, and launched myself without looking down below—focusing only on what Gerald called . . . the lifeline. I honestly thought I was going to see my entire life flash before my eyes, but instead, I heard myself shout out something I would've never thought possible:

Champ Camp is awesoooooome!

WAAIAIAHOOOOO!

It was such an amazing feeling!

  I really handled it like a pro—I wasn't scared at all! And before I could even think about it, I was already on the other side with Anthony and Kader, who took my equipment and sent it back to the rest of the group.

  That's when I noticed that, back on the other side, there was an argument between Aldo, Clara, and Valentin. From the way they were grabbing at the pulley, it looked like they all wanted to be the one to cross right after me. I think Mehdi and Nico were trying to calm them down, but Clara ended up winning and came flying straight into my arms. Valentin followed, and he flew straight into my arms as well. I guess I got more than I bargained for.

Next Aldo threw himself across, yelling, "I'm-a the prankmaster!" But two seconds later, disaster struck! He got stuck in the middle of the traverse . . . right over the gap! 😲 Let's just say he immediately went from laughing to crying, and he started flailing wildly in an attempt to move the pulley forward.

Save me! I broke-a my-a aldocep!

I was a little worried for him, but I suddenly remembered the advice from *Dindin Hood's Journal.* I cupped my hands around my mouth and first tried to calm Aldo down. Then I explained how he could climb back up the pulley. If he turned along the cable so that his back faced the intended direction, putting his arms as far behind his head as possible would make his body parallel with the cable and move him backward slow and steady. That's exactly what was written in Dindin's notebook—he's seriously a lifesaver! For the first time in nearly two weeks, Aldo, this first-class troublemaker, listened to instructions. He was able to get back to where he started to try zipping across again . . . scared to death, but at least with more momentum this time.

Then we cheered on everyone else who joined us one by one, yelling things like:

I'm alive!

We did it!

I'm flying!

This is sick!

When Nico arrived on his turn, he nodded to me and whispered that I'd done a good job with Aldo. Without me, that wimp could've said "ciao" to this cruel world!

It must have been late, because the sun was already starting to set. Luckily, the "extraction point" was only ten minutes away, and we were super relieved to see the buildings of Champ Camp appear in the distance.

We all joined hands, I raised our totem
pole up high, and we ran all the way back to
camp. 😃 We were finally back to our camp!
Before heading to the dining hall with the
others, Aldo came to see me. He wanted to
talk man to man, one on one.

DAY 14
Friday

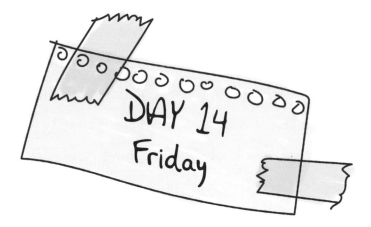

Dear future
human,

It's super late at the time I'm writing this. Today was our last full day at camp, and the schedule was packed. Tomorrow, we'll get back on the bus and return to our homes. And after everything we'd just gone through together, the mood was a little glum. 🙂

We spent part of the morning summarizing and discussing the backpacking trip and camp in general. Nathan, the brainy kid, 🤓 said that, "broadly speaking, camp was a slice of life that will enrich his future." Samuel said this was his best year at camp yet, but it was his last because he's too old to come back again. Lola

totally loooOOved it!

LIKE SO MUCH!

For his part, Nico wasn't sorry he came (and me, neither!). Romain gave the dining hall five stars. Killian added that he was "stoked to come back next year." Aldo admitted he'd made some real friends at camp, and even Valentin said he'd "grown up a lot" over the last two weeks.

Anthony gave me the talking stick and asked if I'd appreciated my vacation after all. I had no choice but to acknowledge that, despite the "bumpy start," I'd really loved the last two weeks at Champ Camp. (◔‿◔) Gerald gave this whole speech about the courage and self-control we'd shown during the wilderness trek, and he told us we were a great group. He passed out a medal to each of us and congratulated everyone. We patted each other on the back 🤚☺ and took a group photo in the middle of camp.

In the dining hall, we had a celebration lunch of chicken, fries, and chocolate cake. All of our free time in the afternoon was spent packing our bags. My roommates and I all swapped our favorite T-shirts, like soccer players after a match. I gave my IAG shirt to Mehdi. All of a sudden, I felt a pillow hit me smack dab on my head. It was Yanis, who'd just provoked a battle from his perch on the top bunk. It was on!

We swung our pillows at each other, as well as the sheets and anything else we could find.

We were cracking up, and when Anthony came to see what all the commotion was about, he took a pillow to the face too. Afterward, we took a little trip to Montlardons to buy some souvenirs for our families.

Tonight was the
BIG GOING-AWAY PARTY!

In the clearing, behind the Champ Camp buildings, we spent the rest of the afternoon decorating the party zone. We hung tinsel, flags, and paper lanterns. Gerald got everything ready for a bonfire. Anthony and Kader handled the sound system. Around seven o'clock, we went back to our rooms to "spruce ourselves up"—even though you've got to admit, dear future human, I never have to do much, thanks to my natural charm.

We put on our Champ Camp shirts but left the hats in our bags. I mean, let's not push it! No way we're going to look dumb for the big party. Aldo even lent us his hair gel and body spray, so much so that we all ended up looking a little bit like him, except for one thing: he put on an earring.

We met up with the girls, who'd all put flowers in their hair. Clara had a little makeup on. She looked really pretty. Lola had gone a little overboard, but Aldo seemed to like it. We pigged out on hotdogs and s'mores cooked over the fire. Gerald played some guitar, and we sang the camp song.

Summer's finally here, now it's time to cheer.
We're here at Champ Camp, so let's stomp and stamp.
We have so much fun, in a blink it's done,
When it's time to go, we'll say "Awww, no!"

We made some friends we'll keep till the end.
We laughed and smiled and slept in the wild.
We'll never forget our best two weeks yet,
But hold back your tears, there's always next year!

Then Anthony and Kader put on the music, and we started dancing. Aldo hit the makeshift dance floor with Lola. Valentin grabbed Lou's hand. Nico got up with Coline, and I'm pretty sure Anthony, the counselor, went out with Caroline . . . the counselor.

Clara and I were sitting right next to each other on a log. 😊 I suggested we go take a little walk, past the clearing. First I apologized for avoiding her a little during camp. I told her I really did think she was sweet and totally gorgeous, but that I had a girlfriend back home and I was the loyal type. I'm still wondering where I pulled all of these lines from.

Clara put her finger over my mouth and said, "Shhhh." I thought she was just about to kiss me anyway, 😙 but that's when we heard the sound of two deafening firecrackers. We looked up at the sky, and it was full of fireworks! 😱 It was Bastille Day, which is the French independence day, kinda like July 4th! Clara took my hand 😉 and led me back to camp, with the others, and we all watched the show. It was really something. The fireworks were almost better than the ones I'd watched in Brittany, to be honest!

Then, since it was a nice night and the sky was clear, Gerald suggested we go get our pillows and blankets so we could sleep under the stars! That was enough to send us rushing back to our rooms. Some people fell asleep right away, others later. Mehdi, Nico, Yanis, Clara, Coline, some others, and I decided to stay up all night to take advantage of the rest of our time.

Later on, when everyone was sound asleep, we gathered together for one last meeting of our mystery council. I had a great idea:

make a survival kit for the next campers and hide it under a bed.

The others thought it was brilliant.

Nico gave me a wink, remembering the one we bury every year in the vacant lot. We slipped away to the kitchen, where we found an empty box in the trash. Jackpot! That would do the trick. Then we all quietly split up to go look for souvenirs around camp that could go in the box. The girls found paper hearts, mascara, and a bag of marshmallows. We threw in the backpacking compass, some advice scrawled on a piece of paper, a can of sardines snatched from the chow hall, a Montlardons postcard, a Champ Camp sun hat, and tons of other stuff. But above all, we added *Dindin Hood's Journal.* It could prove to be extremely useful for other people.

Then before hiding the survival box under my bed, we all made a pact:

to come back next year!

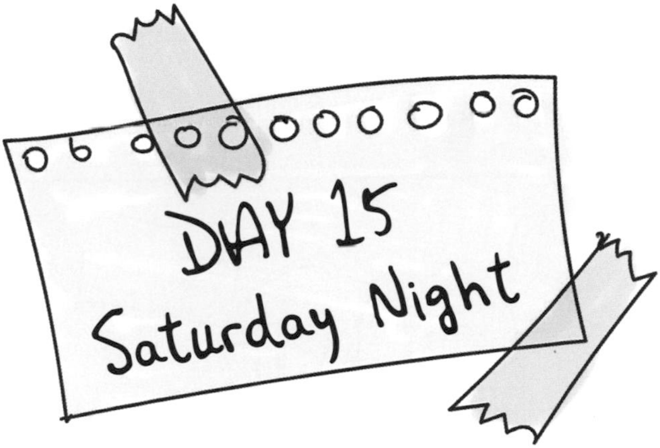
DAY 15
Saturday Night

Dear future  human,

Here I am, back at home. I'm reunited with my parents, my sisters, my room, my video games, and my furry blanket. There was even a little present waiting on my desk.

It's all good, and life is smooth. You'd think I'd be relieved to get back safe and sound, that I'd consider myself some kind of survivor from now on—a true adventurer, even a hero!

And yet ever since the bus stopped, I got off, and said goodbye to everyone, I've been feeling pretty bummed. Before going our separate ways, we all hugged and exchanged addresses and phone numbers. We cried, OK, I admit it.

I got in the car and stuck my nose against the rear window, waving goodbye. I saw them shrink into the distance—spots, black smudges, a single point, then nothing. It was clear that camp was really over. Yeah, OK, I know you must be telling yourself I'm never happy. For two weeks, day by day, hour by hour, minute by minute, I was dreaming of only one thing: escaping that rotten prison and never setting a single toe in camp again.

But in the end, I've gotta say, camp turned out to be really . . .

GREAT!

I made new friends there; I survived, even without candy, salt and vinegar chips, and video games; I even spent the night with a girl—well technically speaking; I met up with Nico, my BFF; I solved the puzzle of *Dindin Hood's Journal*; and I think with all the survival stuff I learned, I became a man . . . mostly. 😊 I'm almost certain I spotted a manly wrinkle on my forehead. Anyway, how can I put it? . . . I have some unforgettable memories. 😊

I already asked my parents to sign me up for next year, and I think it'll work out. At least they didn't say no—that's something. 🙂 There's only one issue: the number of days I have to cross off before I go back is unbelievable. Dear future human, to whoever is now reading these desperately scrawled lines: (take me back!) I don't know if I can hold out that long.

FIND MAX'S
PREVIOUS ADVENTURES!

BOOK 1

Max only dreams of one thing: leaving his mark on history and becoming the hero of his era! Well, OK, at the moment he's only going into sixth grade. . . . But between Naïs, his secret crush, Raoul, his worst enemy, and the English exchange students, the year doesn't look like a walk in the park!

BOOK 2

This year, there's no doubt: Max has got this! His main goal? Get closer to Naïs. And he has just the idea in mind to do it! But the arrival of Nico, the new kid, and his enrollment in Reading Passion club aren't going to make things easier. . . .

ANNE KALICKY

Passionate reader and serial scribbler since the age of seven, one day Anne decided to grow up a bit and "blend in," become an editor, and eventually start writing for herself. It's the only credible  (or not) disguise she could find to pretend to be an adult. Anne is a sensitive, optimistic daydreamer with a smile always on her face, kind of like her character.

TIM JONES

Tim Jones was six when he drew his first Smiley face. Created as an act of rebellion on the wall  of his cafeteria, the Smiley wore a huge grin, had large open eyes, and was farting. Today, Tim lives in London, loves tea, and constantly eats cereal (for breakfast, lunch, and dinner). When he's not drawing, he plays tennis, runs marathons from time to time, listens to music, and DJs in his spare time.

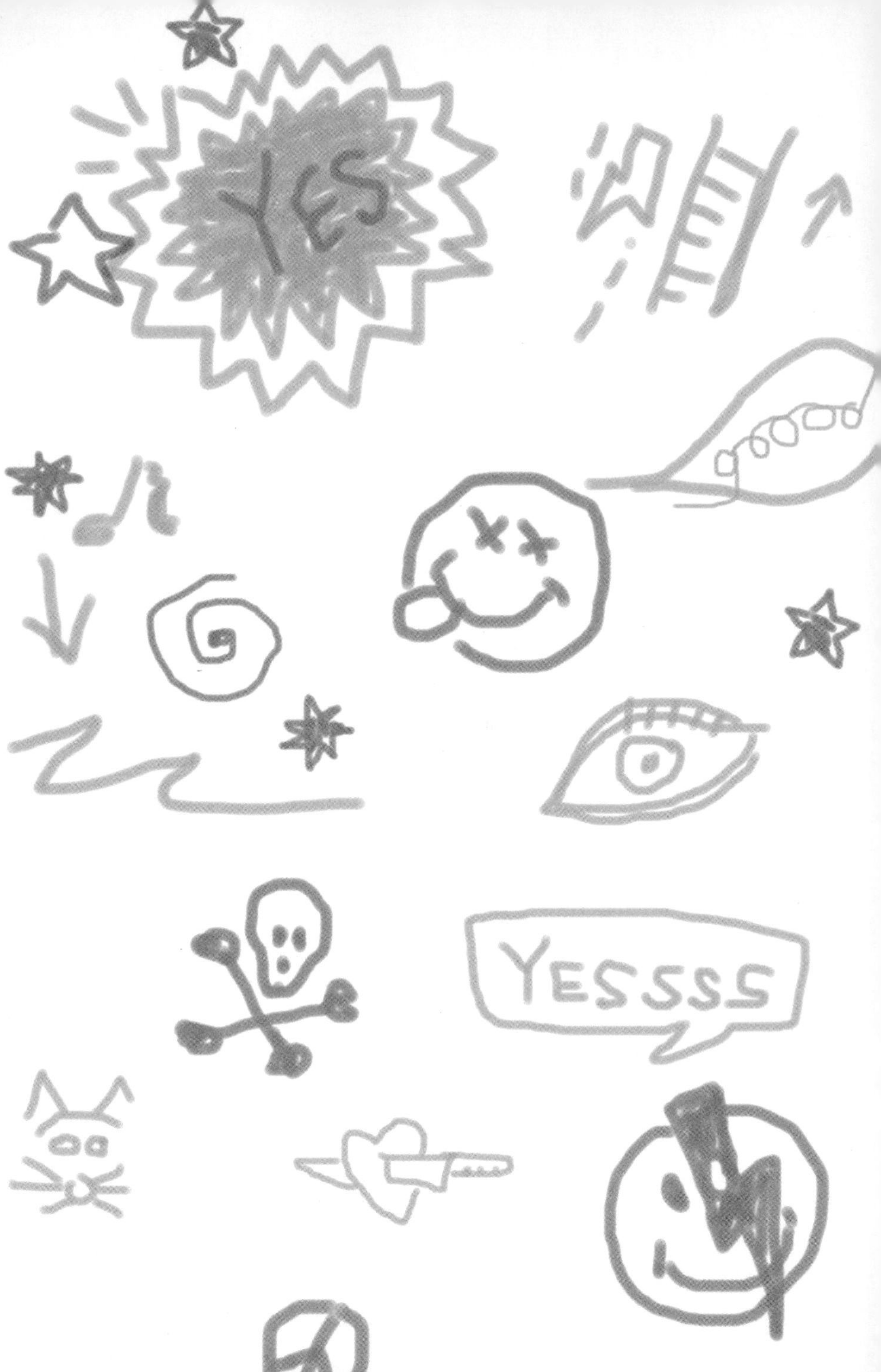

YES
YESSSS

Andrews McMeel Publishing
a division of Andrews McMeel Universal
1130 Walnut Street, Kansas City, Missouri 64106

www.andrewsmcmeel.com

19 20 21 22 23 SDB 10 9 8 7 6 5 4 3 2 1
ISBN: 978-1-4494-9572-5
Library of Congress Control Number: 2018966021

Made by:
Shenzhen Donnelley Printing Company Ltd.
Address and location of manufacture:
No. 47, Wuhe Nan Road, Bantian Ind. Zone,
Shenzhen, China, 518129
1st Printing—2/11/19

Editor: Jean Z. Lucas
Art Director/Designer: Diane Marsh
Production Manager: Chuck Harper
Production Editor: Margaret Daniels
Translator: Kevin Kotur

ATTENTION: SCHOOLS AND BUSINESSES
Andrews McMeel books are available at quantity discounts with
bulk purchase for educational, business, or sales promotional use.
For information, please e-mail the Andrews McMeel Publishing
Special Sales Department: specialsales@amuniversal.com.